THE NARCISSIST'S WIFE

Also by Laura Mansfield

Geezer Stories: *The Care and Feeding of Old People*

The
NARCISSIST'S
Wife

Laura Mansfield

WordCrafts

The Narcissist's Wife is a work of fiction. a work of fiction. Names, characters, businesses, events, and incidents are the products of the author's imagination. Any resemblance to actual persons, living or dead, or actual events is purely coincidental.

The Narcissist's Wife
Copyright © 2019
Laura Mansfield

Cover concept and design by David Warren.

Published by WordCrafts Press
Cody, Wyoming 82414
www.wordcrafts.net

For Mac.

"Be okay with your past. It's brought you to the magic of now."
—Dana Damara

Courtship
&
Seduction

"How to begin? It all seems so obvious now—with the hyperclarity of hindsight.

I imagine this is what it must feel like to have cataract surgery and suddenly the smudged glass of your eyeballs is wiped clean with Windex, and you have that *aha* moment. Yup, that's exactly how it feels to marry a narcissistic sociopath disguised as Mr. Right.

Of course, if we're being honest here—and let's do—my gut always said something was off. *Trust your gut*, they say. Your inner knowing. Your animal instinct. But I was a wounded animal, staggering through the woods with my heart bleeding right out of my chest. I couldn't hear my gut whispers over the deafening din of my hemorrhaging heart.

I mean, I was holding that damaged organ like a wad of wet newspapers in both hands, trying to go on for the sake of my son. I couldn't eat, couldn't sleep, had lost weight. Had hipbones *and* collarbones again that I hadn't seen since high school. I was accidentally erasing myself. Something had to change.

Friends convinced me to try online dating. *It's not just for losers*, they assured me. *This is the digital age.*

I thought it would be just to get my feet wet, to tiptoe into the shallow end of dating and get my mind off the severed limb that was my previous relationship. I had to find a way to numb that phantom pain and quench the sense of longing for something that's gone for good.

I would be a digital dating dilettante. Just dabbling. Nothing serious.

So, I made my profile, didn't overthink it. Just pulled my bio from Twitter and added a few pics from Facebook. I think I chose a photo of my red cowboy boots. And a sweet snapshot of my dog, Hank. Also, a picture I'd taken during a recent yoga retreat in the Guatemalan Highlands.

Next thing you know I was swept up into a dating vortex of coffee at Starbucks, wine at chic little bistros, and one bad-breathed brunch at the local crêperie, where the guy actually wanted to *split* a savory crêpe and ordered one dish for the both of us. It seemed presumptuous. And cheap. And overly familiar for a blind date. And I'm sweet, not savory.

He later texted me pictures of his daughter's new kitten.

Then I met Mike, and I liked him right away because his name was Mike, which is my son's name, so I said something cheesy like, *I've never met a Mike I didn't like.* And he had kind eyes in the picture, nice laugh crinkles around them. And I had also said, "Hair optional—Sense of humor mandatory" in my preferences, because guys get too hung up about thinning hair and forget about being funny and warm and kind. They also forget about abs and get big squishy middles too, but that's another story. And who needs hair anyway? I mean not Jason Statham, right? He doesn't have time for hair. He's too busy having washboard abs.

Anyway, Mike had hair, so whatever. Longish, actually, and he was rather vain about it, always running his hands through it and tossing it back like a schoolboy's wayward bang. It was an affectation, I realize now. And it bugged me even then, but I was trying not to judge him for little things. Like always answering his phone whenever it rang with, "Dr. Pazzo here" or "This is Dr. Michael Pazzo" in his best TV anchorman voice, emphasis on the word "doctor." And he wasn't even a *real* doctor—as in MD. Pazzo was a PhD, a forensic neuropsychologist actually, which he would manage to work into the first sentence or two of meeting anyone.

Red flag.

Narcissists, or people with narcissistic personality disorder (NPD), are prone to bragging, subtly but persistently, and exaggerating their achievements. Self-aggrandizement is not just a quirk, it's a core personality trait of narcissists.

Online he messaged me—"Your face is beautiful, but I wonder what your laugh sounds like?" And that made me smile a shy smile to myself and decide he might be worth meeting.

We met for lunch at a favorite spot of mine. Quiet, elegant, white tablecloths, frequented by businessmen on expense accounts and ladies who *lunch*. I saw an oldish, but not quite vintage, silver Jaguar parked conspicuously in front of the restaurant. Making a statement. Not discreetly situated a space or two to the left or right. Smack dab in front of the door, so you couldn't miss it. My heart sank a little. *So, he's one of those guys*, I thought, pining momentarily for my lost love, who drove a beat-up Jeep full of dog Frisbees and yoga mats.

Then I squared my shoulders, took a deep breath and walked in anyway.

He was seated at a corner table, dressed in a boxy suit, wearing a big, expensive watch of some sort. And cuff links, like an '80s stockbroker. Phone face up on the table beside him. He grinned from ear to ear and said, "You're *gorgeous*," in a sort of faux-gangster James Cagney voice. And he listed to the left all through lunch. Literally. Like he was a little off balance. I realized later he must be somewhere on the spectrum for Asperger's, just like his son, who would become my stepson and my all-consuming responsibility, in addition to my own son, my job, my elderly parents and, of course, my churlish husband. But that was later.

Pazzo sort of leaned to one side and kept the conversation light and lively and sprinkled with compliments. He had this way of looking at me like I was the only person in the room. High beams on. He was scanning for information, memorizing me, cataloging my every feature and random comment, storing it away to use later against me. But I didn't know that then.

I just thought he was really into me and maybe I still had "it," despite being dumped by the love of my life *and* having just turned 50. That was part of it, too. It was a new year—my birthday's in January, so it always takes on extra significance for me—and I was starting a new chapter of my life. Dating. Getting back in circulation. Getting my braces off. Did I mention I had adult braces? I know, right? I think I should get a gold star for effort for going on blind dates while wearing braces.

I was just back from Paris, where I celebrated my milestone birthday, so we talked about that. And I really can't remember

4

what else. Was probably worried about getting food in my braces the whole time. Did I have wine? Not sure. So, *blah, blah, blah,* we had lunch, and he roared off in his big-ass Jag, already talking on the phone, after having taken several "urgent" calls during lunch (I turned my ringer off and kept my phone in my purse). This was five years ago when mobile devices weren't quite as ubiquitous, and even I hadn't started obnoxiously Instagramming my food, which I would do later in the relationship, much to Pazzo's chagrin.

He had mentioned something about meeting friends for dinner that evening and how he'd love for me to come. I was noncommittal but strangely flattered. I hadn't experienced this kind of full-court press from a man in a while. I thought maybe he was smitten. And maybe that was enough for both of us.

He called later from the restaurant with his friends and turned on the charm faucet again.

"Hello gorgeous, I've got your martini waiting, please come," he whispered urgently into the phone. I could hear the din of diners in the background.

But it was raining, and I'd just gotten home from work and was exhausted from having had three dates with three different guys already that week. Match.com don't play, y'all. These men are eager. Dating was becoming a second full-time job, and I was trying to regain my mojo with a steady stream of admirers.

Pazzo had made a big deal at lunch describing his Gibson martini, with a pearl onion in it instead of an olive. *Monkey 47. Gibson. Up.* It was his signature drink, I would come to find out. And I soon learned how to make it just to impress him. Bought a shaker and a special martini glass that I kept in the freezer so his drinks would always be perfectly chilled. Stocked his favorite Monkey 47 gin in my liquor cabinet. It's like I became some 1950s suburban housewife version of myself. But that was later.

This was the martini he was mentioning on the phone, and I was charmed that he had actually ordered a drink for me on the off chance that I might join him.

I declined his rather persistent invitation, and I can't remember what our next date was. But there was a cadence to it all. Texts, calls, drinks, dinner, flowers. He was courting me, as if according to a rom-com script.

Pazzo had this high-pitched girly giggle that unsettled me. Sort of manic. He would burst into it to punctuate his own jokes and anecdotes, as if to cue the audience when to laugh. His silly falsetto guffaws got on my nerves. But I pushed that annoyance down and pleaded with myself to give him a chance and quit being so picky. The man was smart, successful (or so he said), and kind (or so I thought)—and he was *crazy* about me.

Red flag.

Narcissists frequently appear to be charming, intelligent and charismatic. They're prone to flattery and attracted to people who praise them for their abilities or socially accept them. It's all part of the cycle of quashing their deep-seated insecurities by demonstrating or verbalizing their own superiority.

"I'm crazy about you, Jennifer," he'd say, looking directly into my soul in that Charles Manson way of his. And I found that strangely comforting. Pazzo wouldn't fall out of love with me and cheat on me with two married women for a year before leaving me for a younger version of myself, like Peter, my ex-boyfriend. He wouldn't lose his way financially and desperately borrow money from my relatives, finally forging my name on a third mortgage to our house, like Steve, my ex-husband and the father of my child.

And he was funny, jolly even. He made me laugh. I needed that.

There was a story he told about working in a Greek restaurant when he was a teenager and how the owner didn't speak much English, and no one who worked there could understand a word he said. He'd rush into the kitchen and yell something that sounded like, "*Uh-Bee-Duh-Bow*," which meant different things to everyone who heard it.

For Pazzo, the command meant to sweep the floor, so he swept furiously, head down and eyes on his broom. For his buddy, Frank, it meant to saw off another serving from the frozen log of chili. For a third kitchen worker, it meant to take out the trash. Pazzo would act out all the roles, from the exasperated restaurant owner to the three employees frantically performing their respective duties. I was particularly delighted by the image of the frozen chili log, and I laughed till tears streamed down my face. Pazzo's elaborate pantomimes never ceased to amuse me.

He was always on. Always performing. Loved being the center of attention—*my* attention. As his rapt audience of one, I was both captive and captivated. Only later would I learn that performance is a sort of protection for narcissists, so they never have to face being themselves.

While I was seeing Pazzo, I was simultaneously dating a non-Match guy I'd recently reconnected with on Facebook. He was a player, and we both knew it. In fact, I called him "playuh" and we laughed about it. He was a confirmed commitment-phobe but hotter than dammit. I had a serious crush on him but knew he'd break my heart. So, I kept the playuh *and* the nice guy, as I referred to Pazzo, when discussing the dating game with my girlfriends, as in, "he's nice, but…"

I was conflicted. And determined to keep my options open. I had always been a serial monogamist, all the way back to high school. Now I was trying to play the field at 50. It was *my* turn to be a *playuh*. I'd gone from boyfriend to boyfriend to husband to boyfriend to alone for the first time in 35 years, and I wanted to enjoy the sensation of being single now that the throbbing of my stomped-on heart was starting to dull a bit. Oh, I could still conjure up the pain if I thought about my ex, or stalked his new love on Facebook, or caught a glimpse of either of them anywhere. Did I mention she was married, too? So, they had this sly, sexy, stealthy, steamy yoga affair going on. Peter had been my guruji as well as my soulmate. And now he was hers.

I'll never forget the day I came home to find his email open on my computer. The thread of torrid messages between him and yoga skank, as I came to refer to her.

"I wish I could wrap you in my love and hold you forever," Peter had said to her. His words were tattooed on the insides of my eyelids, seared into my brain. I couldn't unsee them.

Now I was trying to distract myself by juggling the playuh and the nice guy. Looking back on it, the playuh actually had integrity, because he told me upfront he was not going to commit or be monogamous. He didn't pretend to be anything he wasn't. I thought I could win him over and liked the challenge of it. Besides, I had the nice guy on a string.

Until he found out about the playuh.

"You mean you're seeing other people?" Pazzo asked in a strangled voice at our Valentine's Day lunch. He looked stricken.

We'd had maybe six dates total. I had brought him a card and a guitar pick and some other guitar gizmo. He fancied himself a songwriter and had a band. He was a neuropsychologist by day and a rock star by night. I forget now how the dating-other-people thing came up. Maybe it was the casual wording of my Valentine. Truth was I had a date planned that night with Playuh, and I was really looking forward to it. He was cooking dinner for me, the first time a man had ever done that. I thought that was very sexy. Was planning to wear this little red lace dress that showed off my yoga-buff arms and grief-induced flat tummy.

Besides, Pazzo had never said anything about being exclusive. We weren't sleeping together. It was just old-fashioned dating with heavy goodnight kissing at the door. After our last date, he had impulsively started kissing my stomach, pulling up my shirt to reveal my bare skin. I was kind of grossed out by this and couldn't help but notice the shiny bald spot on the top of his head.

But in general, he was a pretty good kisser. Although he was prone to moaning my name, which seemed like bad acting to me, like he was starring in his own personal soft-porn soap opera. Was this all just a performance, and a lousy one at that? I would sometimes find myself watching us kiss from outside myself, a detached observer, an innocent bystander.

I couldn't shake that feeling of being a spectator in our relationship. An onlooker, rather than an active participant, observing myself. Narrating my life instead of living it. I was never in the moment with Pazzo.

It was as though I was staring at the screen in the dark but without the popcorn. And the performance wasn't moving me, which was disappointing. I wanted to *feel* something, to get swept up in the story of *us*. But it didn't feel real or authentic. Pazzo was acting, playing the role of adoring boyfriend, crazy about me, when he was actually just plain crazy.

He called two nights later and broke up with me. Told me he had decided to date someone else who was ready to be exclusive, and so he no longer wished to see me. He was very businesslike and perfunctory about it. Like he was dismissing a temporary employee or sending back undercooked salmon at dinner. He had turned off all emotion with the flip of a switch. I assumed his flat affect was a cover for his hurt pride, that he was trying to maintain control of his emotions—*emotional blunting*, I think it's called. After all, this was such a shift from his excessively amorous behavior, to which I'd become slightly addicted, like vending machine candy, not your favorite kind but it's convenient, so you eat it anyway.

How do you go from adoration to apathy in the blink of an eye? Ask a narcissist.

He didn't ask me how I felt about it or say he was sorry. He was simply informing me of his decision. His tone was clipped and terse. No flowery words or high-pitched giggles. This was a glimpse of the real Mike Pazzo. Heartless, soulless, manipulative, and mean. But I was naïve then. I'd never dated a true narcissist. Sure, my exes were self-centered, but aren't all men? I grew up Southern and female, raised to sublimate my needs, putting other people first, particularly men.

This was different. It was chilling. Like he was a robot. Or a stranger. And he was.

Red flag.

Narcissists have difficulty with empathy. They are incapable of

feeling and understanding the emotions of others. Narcissists detest
those who do not admire them. If you don't drink their Kool-Aid,
you'll be quickly rejected and replaced by someone who does.

"Um, okay," I stammered, since he had caught me off guard,
and I was slightly stunned. I may have even cried a little, just
from hurt feelings and the meanness of it. He was breaking
up with me when we weren't actually dating each other. Was
that even a thing? Was he trying to salvage his fragile ego by
getting out of the relationship before he got hurt? Or was
this a calculated quid pro quo for inadvertently hurting his
feelings on Valentine's Day?

I wasn't sure.

When he texted out of the blue a month later, I was
circumspect.

It was three words: "Dinner Saturday night?"

Hmm. It was a Tuesday, so the timing was good. I didn't
have a date for Saturday yet. Can't remember what was up
with Playuh. We didn't see each other every week. Our relationship was still super casual, despite Valentine's Day dinner
and the red lace dress, which had ended up on the floor.

My expat friend Monika, who had accompanied me on
my birthday jaunt to the City of Lights, said in her charming
Swiss accent, "Why do you not give the nice guy another
chance?" She didn't know he was a monster in disguise. She
only knew he had wined me and dined me and sent me
roses at work and brought me chocolates on Valentine's Day.
Not dark chocolate and not Godiva, but I was trying to be
non-judgmental, remember? And she and I both knew there
was no future with Playuh.

It was March by now, and my son and I were on a college-
visiting road trip for spring break. I was driving when Pazzo's

text popped up on my phone. I let it marinate for an hour or so, not wanting to reply too quickly and not really sure whether or not I wanted to see him again. Little voices inside me were making anxious agitated sounds, warnings of some sort, but I didn't recognize them at the time.

He hurt you on purpose. Red flag.

And then Monika's words popped back into my head, and I ignored my inner guardian angels.

Why do you not give the nice guy another chance?

I thought maybe I was avoiding commitment in order not to be hurt again, and that was why I had been hesitant to be exclusive with Pazzo. I chalked up his weird break-up call to his machismo. He was half-Sicilian, and a friend had told me that Italian men are overly sensitive to perceived slights. She was, herself, an East Tennessee girl, married to a proud, first-generation Italian American from Chicago.

Anthony Michael Pazzo, aka Mike, aka Dr. Pazzo, aka Dr. Michael Pazzo was *very* Italian in his sensibilities. Later I would learn he had gone by yet another name—Tony Pazzo— in his previous life in Detroit before reinventing himself in Cherokee Hills. Turns out, I really knew very little about him.

But I figured if he wanted to see me again, I'd give him a chance to make it up to me. Maybe try dating *just* him and see where it led. After all, I reasoned, he was a nice guy. Wasn't he?

How to describe Mike Pazzo, physically, I mean. *Hmm.* It's difficult to separate the physical from the intellectual, because his intellect was intense, like the sharp edge of an expensive carving knife. And before he emotionally flayed me over and over, he charmed me with his cutting wit and clever banter. I'm a sucker for a smart guy. Have always prided myself on being more into the person than the appearance of the person. And that was definitely true in Pazzo's case.

He was roundish, heavy-set with slightly bulging eyes, like a bullfrog. But there was something about his fleshy jaw and the laugh lines around his eyes that showed a flash of what once was. Not a beautiful man, but perhaps he had been a beautiful boy? Not conventionally beautiful, because I later saw pictures of him as a teenager, dressed all in black, gazing lovingly at his guitar through Coke-bottle glasses (He'd since had LASIK surgery).

Maybe I needed to think Pazzo had once been sweet and vulnerable—with an inner beauty and an actual soul. This version of him fit the narrative I was constructing in my head to explain his cruel alter ego. He had been hurt and was only trying to protect himself. I was projecting, of course, and rationalizing my need to save him. I collected broken people like the torn paper dolls I'd taped back together and kept in a box when I was a child. I couldn't bear to throw them away.

"I hate the way I look now," he'd complain, when catching a glimpse of himself in the mirror. "I don't even recognize myself anymore. I look like my uncles who all look like Fred Flintstone."

In retrospect, when I deconstruct his features, I can't come up with anything attractive. Thinning, too-long-for-his-age hair— mouse colored, somewhere between brown and gray. Small, square teeth like Chiclets. Thin lips. Saggy face melting into his collar like a scoop of stubbly vanilla ice cream. And a bad case of man boobs. Moobs. Very unappealing. With wiry hairs around nipples the size of silver-dollar pancakes.

Pazzo had pale, pinkish skin (he hated the sun). In fact, he was sort of Porky Piggish, in both shape and color. Except for his feet, which were even paler and also moist. Like a salamander.

He never took his shoes off. Ever. Couldn't walk barefoot in the grass. I thought he was kidding about it, until I noticed his son Marco suffered from the same affliction, a hypersensitivity to surfaces and changes in temperature, an aversion to warmth, like they were cave dwellers, Gollums from a mythical kingdom.

But Pazzo joked about it, saying that his first wife—his "real" wife—as he referred to Angela to distinguish her from Ivy, his second wife, Marco's mother, whom he detested and vilified at every opportunity, had never actually seen his feet in 10 years of marriage. So, we laughed about his peculiar foot fetish, his aversion to his own feet.

He was hairy too. Back hair on fleshy shoulders like a pallid primate. Pazzo recalled that Marco once asked if he could play with his father's back fat. Still makes me laugh. Pazzo's self-deprecating humor was disarming. I thought it indicated that he didn't take himself too seriously. Only now I think it masked his deep self-loathing, which drove his insatiable need to collect things—cars and guitars—and women, like me, to externally validate his self-worth. In fact, he once told me I was shaped like a guitar. Yes folks, I was destined to be a tarnished trophy wife.

Pazzo's dad, Alfredo Pazzo, had immigrated from Sicily as a child, with his grieving father, who had recently married his dead wife's sister, in some sort of old-world custom that sounded made up to me. Alfredo had two sets of siblings. One that shared the same mother and father and then one that only shared a father. He was in the first batch that settled in an Italian neighborhood of Detroit. Alfredo fell in love with a girl from a Scottish neighborhood, Lorna Lee or Lorna Doone or something like that. A shortbread cookie with copper hair and hazel eyes.

Pazzo told me that Italian men of his father's generation were always looking for a *Colleen*, a fair-skinned Irish or Scots girl, as their ideal beauty, having grown up among olive-skinned, licorice-haired women. Lorna was Alfredo's *Colleen*. And he had loved her since he was 12 years old. He worked odd jobs—including delivering papers and killing rats—to save up the money to buy his sweetheart a silver tea service when he was only 15. Alfredo Pazzo never felt good enough for Lorna, whose family looked down on him, and he spent his life trying to prove his worth. Lorna died a couple of years before I met Pazzo, and I couldn't help but feel like I was Pazzo's *Colleen*.

We made the pilgrimage to Michigan to meet Alfredo Pazzo, who was retired from the auto industry, after having worked for GM for decades. Alfredo didn't have a college degree, but he was an engineer at heart and worked his way up through the ranks, ultimately inventing the inter-mittant windshield wiper because his beloved Lorna hated the squeeky sound the blades made when the glass wasn't constantly wet. At least that's what Pazzo claimed. I don't know if that's true, but it made a charming story. It seemed there was nothing Alfredo wouldn't do for his dream girl.

Lorna had been an invalid for many years, suffering from nebulous maladies before she died, and Alfredo had lovingly cared for her right up until the end. Pazzo would recall, some-what bitterly, having to play quietly as a child, so as not to disturb his frail mother who was always *resting*.

I liked Alfredo right off. He had his son's easy charm but without the hard edges.

"Tell me about *you*, Jennifer," he began, when we sat down in his suburban living room, Pazzo's sister Sophie perched beside him. They both called Mike "Tony" from time to time, before catching themselves and switching to "Mike."

When I asked him about the name thing, Pazzo said it was customary in Italian families to have one name your family calls you and then a different name you use when you're not at home. He was "Tony" at home and "Anthony" at school. Which didn't explain how or when he had become "Mike," but I let it drop.

Sophie was the new invalid in the family, Alfredo's project now that Lorna was gone. She had moved home to help care for her mother and now suffered from a range of emotional disorders—anxiety, depression, anorexia—and Alfredo was supervising her meds. There was clearly some dysfunction here. Alfredo was a caretaker, and he needed to be in control. Just like his son.

Munchausen syndrome by proxy, perhaps? MSBP is a form of abuse in which the caretaker makes up fake symptoms or causes real symptoms to make it look like the child is sick, thereby raising the parent's status (I did the googles). I would come to recognize this same pattern of behavior in Pazzo's relationship with Marco, and, to a certain extent, with Ivy.

There was an older brother, Alfredo Jr., who was estranged from the family, but was clearly Pazzo's idol. The way he told it, Alfie had disowned his family when he married a wealthy WASP from Grosse Point, because he was embarrassed of his working-class parents. And later, he had cut off all contact with Pazzo, his adoring kid brother, once Alfie and his wife had their own children. Pazzo felt abandoned by his big brother, who was by then a big, important tax attorney at a Fortune 500 company.

Alfie had been a musical prodigy as a child, attending the prestigious Interlochen Arts Academy on scholarship. Pazzo would follow in his brother's footsteps, earning a poetry scholarship to spend his senior year of high school at Interlochen, where he met a quirky redhead from Tennessee, named Ivy, who would become Marco's mother many years later.

Pazzo and Ivy weren't friends at Interlochen. Apparently Ivy smoked so much weed that they gave her a private room at the end of a hall, so the ubiquitous clouds wafting under her door wouldn't bother the other residents at the posh boarding school. Ivy was a stoner, artsy and angry. She and Mike—or maybe it was Anthony then—ran in different circles.

But they would bump into each other decades later at an Interlochen reunion. Pazzo, recently divorced and lonely would hook up with Ivy that weekend. At 40-something, she became pregnant with his child. Pazzo, whose first marriage had ended, in part due to infertility problems, was thrilled to be a father at last and followed Ivy back to Tennessee.

Okay, time out, you have to ask yourself, *why a successful neuropsychologist would leave a thriving practice in Michigan to relocate to Cherokee Hills, Tennessee, where his deadbeat wife wrote a monthly art column for the local hippie periodical. Why didn't Ivy move to Michigan?*

Because maybe life wasn't as idyllic as Mike Pazzo described it? And maybe he wanted a fresh start in a new town where nobody knew Tony Pazzo.

Red flag. Red flag.

Pazzo and Ivy's romance was whirlwind and long-distance.

They met for romantic weekends in Asheville, Chicago, and New York, where he claimed to have lived for several years, hobnobbing with the literati and musical elite of Manhattan. That was after he came back from London, where he said he also lived for several years. I forgot when or why.

Piecing together the snippets they both shared and stitching those together with my own observations, I can vividly imagine the crazy patchwork quilt of their courtship. Ivy dressed in black, drinking whiskey, and chain-smoking. Pazzo, horny and distracted, at loose ends and restless, like a shark swimming in the water between kills. I'm certain they fought and broke up endlessly. Maybe there was great make-up sex.

Undoubtedly, they hurled vile insults at each other like Molotov cocktails. Their relationship was not a peaceful one. They did not complement or complete each other. One of them was gasoline; the other was the match. Together they were Explosive. Volatile. Deranged. Passionate. Exciting. Unhinged. Combustible. That's how I picture it. They were two magnets, repelled and drawn to each other.

Pazzo didn't actually move to East Tennessee until after Marco was born. Marco grew into a wobbly, red-headed boy, with rabbit teeth and ruby lips, long-limbed like his mother, entirely unlike his fireplug father. Marco had delicate hands with spider-leg fingers, nothing like Pazzo's biscuit dough hands and Vienna-sausage fingers. In fact, father and son had very little in common. Except for the undiagnosed Asperger's, which was painfully obvious in Marco by the time I met him several years later.

Did I mention Ivy was actually living with another guy while she was carrying on her long-distance affaire de coeur with Dr. Pazzo? The roommate relationship was platonic,

Pazzo insisted. But then he was determined to be a father, so he was ready to believe whatever Ivy told him. And Ivy was ready to be a kept woman, underwritten by Pazzo's lucrative practice, tired of slumming it, and eager to return to the idyllic neighborhood of our shared childhood.

Turns out I knew Ivy in elementary school. She lived for a time in Cherokee Hills, where I grew up. Her father was a professor of architecture at the nearby university, her mother a homemaker. Ivy was my brother's age, a grade behind me. After elementary school, she briefly attended the private prep school from which I graduated—when she was still rolling up at Interlochen. I vaguely remembered her from riding the same school bus. We were both clad in navy cardigans, kilts, and saddle shoes, our shared private school uni. Ivy had been skinny and freckled with carrot-colored hair, a Molly Ringwald lookalike from "Sixteen Candles" and "The Breakfast Club." An honest-to-God Colleen like her future mother-in-law, Lorna Pazzo.

We weren't exactly friends in school but growing up in Cherokee Hills gave us a shared past. So, when Ivy dropped off Marco at Pazzo's house in our old neighborhood, which Pazzo somehow got to keep after their divorce, Ivy and I were cordial to each other in the way of old acquaintances reconnecting after many years. Marco, who was 10 or so by then, bounded out of Ivy's car and threw himself into his father's arms like he was still a toddler. It was disconcerting because he was tall for his age, gangly like his mother had been as a child, in his flood-length too-short jeans. Pazzo scooped him up, cutting a sidelong glance at me to make sure

I was clocking this Kodak moment of perfect fatherhood. He took Marco inside for a snack, leaving Ivy and me to chat in the driveway.

"Mike's a narcissist," she blurted at me as soon as he and Marco were out of earshot.

Surprised by this seemingly out-of-context revelation, I looked at her blankly, searching her still-freckled face for some sort of reason for this abrupt disclosure.

"No, *really*," she insisted, nodding her head fervently. "He's been diagnosed and everything."

"You should run while you still can," Ivy advised, looking over her shoulder just as the screen door flew open and Marco darted out like a dragonfly, zig-zagging across the driveway to alight in his mother's still-running car, where he proceeded to play with the steering wheel, making *zoom-zoom* noises.

Ivy and Mike were oblivious to their child. Now that Pazzo's fatherliness had been fully on display for me, he and Ivy were going at it, arguing over something, loudly with the exaggerated gesticulations of cartoon characters. They were lost in their toxic tirade. As their voices rose in volume, so did Marco's car noises. "Zoom zoom *Zoom Zoom!*" he screamed frantically, jerking the steering wheel and rocking back and forth.

I reached inside the driver's side window and turned off the ignition, taking the keys as I did so, lest Marco accidentally put the car in reverse and slide down the steep driveway into the busy street below while his parents spewed vitriol at each other.

"She's *crazy*," Pazzo told me later over a Monkey 47 Gibson at one of our favorite watering holes. "I'm sorry you had to witness that display," he added, shaking his head in disgust.

"What were you and Poison Ivy talking about while I was inside with Marco," he asked casually, twirling the pearlescent onion on the toothpick in his cocktail.

"She told me you were a certifiable narcissist," I answered without hesitation. "Gosh, it was so weird, out of nowhere. Why would she tell me that?"

"Ivy suffers from borderline personality disorder," Pazzo answered, switching smoothly into clinician mode. "She's erratic and unstable. Did I tell you she once threw a soda can at me while I was holding Marco when he was a baby? It was a full can, and it almost hit my head. She never bonded with him. Refused to nurse him. Postpartum depression. I had to be both mother and father to him."

This was a story I'd heard before. On our very first date actually. I hadn't picked up on Pazzo's pious tone at the time, didn't know how he cherished his martyr status as a single dad, even though the ink was not yet dry on his divorce papers. He drank his own bathwater as he warmed to his favorite topic—himself—as father, long-suffering, misunderstood husband of neglectful, possibly even abusive wife. No doubt it played well on his Match dates, earning him solicitous nods and pats, maybe even sympathy sex. But not from me, as I had been a single mom for a decade by then.

"Cry me a river," I had replied instinctively. I meant it in the sense of *tell me something I don't already know*, or *yes, I know what that feels like*, but it came out more harshly than I had intended. I was put off by his faux-victim mentality.

This time I just sighed, but I saw something shift in his eyes, along with a slight flare of his nostrils. He managed to keep his composure, smoothly redirecting his anger at me toward our hapless server.

21

"You call this a Gibson," he roared at the pimply-faced college kid, barely older then my son. "Look at that and tell me why the glass isn't full."

Pazzo pushed back from the table and crossed his arms over his ample girth.

"Sir, that's the way the bartender made it…" our server replied, his gumball-sized Adam's apple bobbing up and down, his voice cracking.

"Does. The. Glass. Look. Full. To. You?" Pazzo demanded indignantly while I looked at my hands and felt terrible for the poor kid.

It was a glimpse at the ugly side of Pazzo that sometimes broke through the surface of his smug façade. He unleashed it relentlessly on Ivy, but generally reined it in around other people. The manager came to our table and explained that the drink had two ounces of gin in it and that the glass was oversized, and the liquid wasn't intended to fill the glass. Our server never came back. They sent a different one to close out our tab.

I was mortified at Pazzo's boorish behavior, having always gone out of my way to be kind and courteous to serving staff and people working in retail. I grew up in a retail family and also in a restrained family where public outbursts were simply not an option. *Manners matter. Nice people don't display their tempers in public and especially don't direct them at people who are in no position to challenge them*, I could hear my mother's voice in my head. By "nice people" she meant "people like us." I had always thought Mom was too self-contained. Now I saw that her constant composure was preferable to Pazzo's bizarre outbursts. He was a bully, plain and simple.

But I let it pass. I did apologize to the server for Pazzo's behavior on my way out. Little did I know I'd soon be the recipient of much worse mercurial outbursts.

In between the barrages of irrational anger there were sweet times, as we tried to find our way together as a couple and gradually include Marco. The child was constantly glued to screens, playing video games that seemed to agitate him like amphetamines. I was always trying to think of ways to unplug him and engage him in the actual world, preferably outdoors.

And, so it was that I planned an excursion to a kitschy and quaint Tennessee tourist destination—Raccoon Mountain Caverns and Campground—a subterranean world with five and a half miles of undergound pathways to explore not far from Chattanooga. I had fond memories of making touristy side trips with my family when I was a kid, Mammoth Cave in Kentucky, for example. I remembered the spooky excited feeling of descending into the dark, surrounded by damp stone walls and strangers. It was thrilling and foreign and otherworldly. I'm sure I took my son on similar field trips when he was little, and we had certainly hiked our share of mountain trails and waterfalls over the years. He was always reluctant to part with his Game Boy but surrendered to his surroundings once we were embraced by ancient moss-covered trees with bear claw marks gouged in the bark. I hoped for a similar experience with Marco.

The 90-minute car ride was tedious, with Marco complaining the whole time. His stomach hurt. He was bored. He was hungry. Could he play with Pazzo's phone? And that classic whine of children on family excursions everywhere since the beginning of time—*Are we there yet? Are we there yet?*

When we arrived at our destination and set foot on the gravel parking lot, Pazzo stretched like a Grizzly after hibernation, arms overhead, hands balled in fists as he emitted a ferocious yawn. Marco did the same. Then Pazzo stood with his right hand on his lower back, left leg forward slightly, staring ahead into the middle distance, getting his bearings. It was a signature pose of his. I found it oddly endearing. I glanced at Marco and noticed he had struck the same pose, which made me smile.

Pazzo began walking toward the ticket booth, as did Marco, who kept his hand on his hip, looking like a little old man with an achy back. Pazzo caught sight of him and snarled, "Why are you walking like that, Marco? You look ridiculous."

"And tie your shoes, for God's sake," Pazzo added before storming away, gravel crunching angrily beneath his feet.

Marco seemed stung by his father's words. He stared at Pazzo through the grimy lenses of his crooked glasses, slack-jawed and pitiful. Finally, he threw both hands in the air and sighed in frustration. I bent over and tied his shoelaces for him and zipped his pants as well, grateful that Pazzo had not noticed his hapless son's open fly or that his Batman undies were on backwards.

We procured our tickets and followed along as the crowd surged forward to the maw of the cavern. As we descended into the darkness, eerily illuminated stalactites hung from the cave ceiling like dragon's teeth, dripping saliva. Most of the group with us was silent in awe, taking it all in, listening to the guide as he told the story of the cave's discovery. At one point we stood in absolute darkness, seeing the caverns as the first explorers did.

The black was so thick you could reach out and grab it like a velvet curtain. Pazzo impulsively grabbed me and kissed me passionately in the inky void, running his hands up my legs, under my skirt. He took my breath away in that moment, when our romance was still new and anything was possible. I felt alive in a way I hadn't for a while. Then the cave lights flickered back on and our guide resumed his narration, interrupted constantly as Marco peppered him with questions.

I was embarrassed by Marco's overly precocious queries and his lack of self-control. Pazzo just gazed at him indulgently, like he was the smartest, most special boy in the world. Father and son were oblivious to the looks of annoyance from the other people on our tour, as well as the exasperation of the tour guide, who had finally started ignoring Marco by simply speaking more loudly to the rest of the group.

In the bowels of the cave we climbed in glass-bottomed boats and paddled across water filled with blind albino fish. I remembered my son's silent fascination with this oddity of nature so many years ago, but Marco seemed more interested in badgering the tour guide with an ongoing barrage of questions. He was desperate to win the approval of the adult authority figure in the group, thereby impressing his own adult authority figure, aka, Pazzo.

When the tour was over, we emerged blinking like moles in the fluorescent lights of the gift shop, Marco was ecstatic, scampering like a squirrel from souvenirs to candy to stuffed animals. We finally dragged him to the snack bar with promises of french fries and Sprite. Pazzo seemed to think as long as a soft drink wasn't dark, it wasn't bad for you.

Marco promptly slurped up three Sprites before bogging down completely on his hamburger, having removed everything but the bun and the meat. I was desperate for him to have something beside sugar and carbs and was peddling burger bites like a drug dealer in a school parking lot.

I don't remember exactly what happened, but Pazzo suddenly erupted like a volcano of crazy and made Marco spit out his partially masticated burger bite into his father's hand. He turned to me angrily and reminded me of Marco's delicate stomach and the fact that his intestines had not been fully formed when he was born and that he subsequently suffered from a litany of digestive issues. Pazzo's eyes were flashing fire as he rebuked me for trying to get Marco to eat the grey meat patty of dubious origin. Marco was delighted to avoid anything even quasi-healthy and sipped his Sprite smugly.

I was left feeling like the rug had been pulled out from under me. Didn't this man just kiss me in the cave? Weren't we in love? And now he was livid because I had encouraged his son to eat his meal. Perhaps I was too familiar with Marco, too eager to co-parent and bond. Pazzo was establishing boundaries, drawing lines in the sand that I was not to cross.

He apologized later, saying he had overreacted. I instantly forgave him.

It was July. We'd been dating for six months. I was still ambivalent about my feelings for Pazzo. But he was steadfast in his adoration of me. And it felt good to be worshiped.

"Thank goodness you never went to Hollywood," Pazzo teased over lunch back at our favorite restaurant—*our* place now since we'd had our first date there. "You would have become the face of a generation, and we would have never met." He was prone to hyperbole, and I enjoyed his playful little paeans, extolling my virtues, a mischievous twinkle dancing in his eye. I could never really tell when he was kidding, but he was always entertaining.

Over coffee and dessert—because he *always* ate dessert— Pazzo pulled out a little black velvet box and put it on the table. My eyes got big as I looked up at him, still making love to his chocolate torte, leaning to the left, fork held sideways.

"Mike, I—"

"It's not what you think. I just wanted you to have this, so you would know that my intentions are honorable," he explained, licking his fingers before opening the box to reveal a diamond solitaire that looked a lot like an engagement ring. I remembered on his Match profile that he had described himself as a gentleman. We'd long since deleted those profiles. At least I had.

I put the ring on my right hand and thanked him, although it really looked like a left-hand ring.

It was typical Pazzo to plan a dramatic moment in front of a crowd. The servers clustered around to *ooh* and *ahh*. There were polite murmurings from nearby tables. A smattering of applause, which Pazzo acknowledged with a wave and a nod.

"In my family, when a man is about to propose to a woman, he gives her a strand of pearls," he said solemnly. "And if she accepts the pearls, then he knows she will accept his marriage proposal."

He was making it clear that there were pearls in my future, but why he felt the need to buy me an engagement ring first was a mystery. And, of course, since he wanted to surprise me, he hadn't asked what kind of ring I'd like, yet somehow his impetuous gesture charmed me. And the ring did make his intentions crystal clear. It legitimized me in my own eyes. I wasn't damaged goods, rejected and cheated on, abandoned and unlovable. A man—a *nice guy*—wanted to marry me. I was redeemed from the ashes of my previous relationship. And I couldn't wait for my ex to hear through the grapevine that I was no longer pining for him.

The irony was not lost on me that I thought of my former lover instead of my current one in that moment.

A word about our sex life, because I know you're wondering.

Let me just say this: Pazzo liked a conquest. Tarzan-style, club a girl over the head, and drag her by her hair back to his cave, figuratively if not literally—but also literally. He was passionate to be sure, and after enduring the waning affections of my cheating boyfriend, I was ready to be ravished. We made love in the moonlight on the hood of his big-ass Jag and later on his Porsche when he tired of his Jaguar and needed a new toy. We'd be outside in the driveway at his house, partially secluded under a canopy of trees and stars, dogs barking and neighbors unaccounted for. It felt daring and naughty. I felt desired.

The Porsche manifested when I casually told Pazzo that my first husband had restored and auto-crossed 911s. "Sliding Steve" they called him on the circuit. Before Mike was born, we'd spent many happy weekends on Sports Car Club and Porsche Club outings, racing around pylons in parking lots and competing in rallies around hairpin curves up in the Smoky Mountains. Steve was a Porsche aficionado. It made my heart hurt to recall Mike as a toddler hearing the familiar rumbling of the engine when Steve came home from work. Our chubby-cheeked toddler would run barefoot across the yard to the driveway where Steve would scoop him up and plop him on his lap so he could "drive" the vintage black 911 into the garage. That car would end up under a tarp in Monika's husband's garage to settle a debt Steve couldn't repay.

So now Pazzo had to have a Porsche, too. And he told me he used to drive Porsches on the Autobahn in Germany and had driven a Porsche Supercar on a professional race track. He had been to racing school, in fact. First I'd heard of this. And I wondered if it was before or after London and New York. Was it while he was racing yachts on Lake Michigan and teaching psychology at Michigan State? Or was it when he had his posh private practice? There were racetracks in Michigan, right? So I guess it was possible. I didn't know the narcissist's illogical need to one-up everyone else. Particularly my ex-husband.

Red flag.

Narcissists often claim to be experts at many things, regardless of the reality of their claims. It's a way of redirecting the topic of conversation back to them and reasserting dominance.

Pazzo and I weren't only having sex on sports cars.

We once became so tousled in the sheets making mad Pazzo-love that I fell out of bed and hit my head on the bedside table, necessitating a trip to the ER and stitches. While I was waiting for the doctor to sew up my face, Pazzo convinced the nurse to take *his* blood pressure, so overwrought was he. Because everything was about him, even the gash on my forehead. He had to be the center of attention. At the time, I thought he was just worried about me and was having heart palpitations due to his extreme devotion.

Our *first time* didn't go so smoothly either. Pazzo had taken me out for an elegant dinner and made a big show of ordering a 50-year-old Scotch. I'm a single-malt girl and an introvert, and while I cringed at his theatrics, I thought it was sweet that he was trying so hard to impress me. I didn't know then that he always needed an audience, that his very existence depended on it.

Marco was with Ivy that night, so we had the evening to ourselves. We went back to his place, which I called "Marco's Playhouse," because it was always littered with broken toys and dirty socks, half-drunk juice boxes and Legos crunching painfully underfoot. I had sensed Pazzo's ardent desire over dinner and thought, *What the hell. Might as well get it over with.*

I shed my little black dress and lay back seductively on his scratchy sofa (he was in between furniture, he explained, Ivy having taken the good stuff). While I was acutely aware of a Star Wars action figure digging into my bare back, I was enjoying my little striptease moment and his obvious appreciation, his uncharacteristic nervousness. I'd been doing a lot of yoga and was pretty confident in my body. The low lighting helped. Also, the expensive Scotch.

He excused himself to the bathroom and walked back in naked and round, like a marshmallow on Tootsie-Roll legs. Ghostly pale and jiggly, as though carved out of Jell-O. I couldn't help but notice.

"You're so beautiful, so perfect," he whispered. "I'm so nervous."

"Don't be nervous," I said automatically, trying to reassure him.

"Just allow me to be nervous. Don't tell me what to do," he snapped.

I lay there and waited until his eyes swelled out of his head like a Looney Tunes character, and his man breasts slapped merrily against his rotund middle. He was both bug-eyed and breathless. Then he suddenly stopped. Something wasn't, umm, working.

Pazzo was mortified at his inability to perform. I tried to make light of it, saying, "It happens sometimes, no worries." But he was grumpy and peevish, taking me home shortly afterwards. I had unwittingly inflicted a narcissistic injury by emasculating him. His impotence was somehow *my* fault.

Red flag. Red flag.

Narcissists are most dangerous when they're emotionally wounded. They're hypersensitive to perceived criticism or the flicker of failure. Humiliation is intolerable for narcissists and must be rectified to demonstrate superiority and regain emotional equilibrium.

We never discussed it. And it never happened again because, I realize now, he started taking male enhancement medications, which stoked his libido and also made his heart rate go up. Later when we were married, he grew even more overbearing and demanding of sex. Spurning his affections was a punishable offense and a dereliction of my wifely duties.

Sex would become a physical need for him and a chore for me. In fact, our intimacy would evolve into sex-on-demand with me as his pliable, ever-ready blow-up doll. I would try to oblige him to avoid his wrath. Over time I grew fearful of his rage and weary of the conflicts he thrived on. I would go along to get along. His mood grew dark as storm clouds when he needed sex but lightened temporarily afterwards. I lived for that short respite, the calm in the eye of the cyclone that was Pazzo, when he was momentarily sated and I could roll over and sleep, unmolested.

I would eventually become a middle-aged Cinderella trapped in a toxic marriage, fixing breakfast and packing lunches for both Pazzo and Marco, who ended up in our full-time custody and care, then cleaning the kitchen and making the bed only to find Pazzo back from dropping Marco off at school and ravenous for sex, his erection visible in his suit pants.

That was to be my life for one miserable year—but I didn't know it then.

As it turned out, Pazzo wanted a mail-order bride, a sex slave/nanny for Marco, not an independent, professional woman who was his equal. He has misrepresented his intentions because to the outside world I was the perfect wife, beautiful in his eyes, blonde, thin, successful in my career with a brilliant son headed off to college to make way for his little broken bird in our nest. I *looked* the part of Mrs. Pazzo. And that's all that ever really mattered.

I know you're thinking; *What the hell, woman? Why did you marry him? Why did you even date him?* But it wasn't as obvious to me then. And there were good times.

At least I think there were.

Or maybe it was just that Pazzo filled a void in my life.

As I close my eyes now and try to conjure up the past through my rose-colored rearview mirror, I remember that Pazzo listened to me—*really* listened. I'll try to explain this in a non-snarky way, stripping off the armadillo shell spiked with porcupine quills I've since grown.

You see, I had felt invisible my whole life, except for those brief shining moments of being in love, of being someone's someone. When Pazzo looked at me with his unwavering gaze and hung on my every word, I felt *seen, heard and understood*. I once heard an early pioneer in social media describe this as the "three-fold human hunger." Trey Pennington was his name, and he attributed the initial rise and success of social media to exactly this phenomenon.

"People just want to be seen, heard and understood."

He later committed suicide.

Sorry, but he did.

When it was just Pazzo and me, maybe sitting on a terrace somewhere, an outdoor patio bar, which was my favorite place to be with him, after a long day at the office, we'd just talk and solve the world's problems, or at least our own. He'd tell me about his work, which endlessly fascinated me and I'd tell him about my day. Pazzo immediately pointed out things I hadn't thought about and helped me glean insights into people's behaviors and motivations. He was good like that. And then he'd make me feel okay about whatever was on my mind or on my heart. Maybe he really *was* a brilliant psychologist. Because in hindsight, it wasn't Pazzo I fell in love with—it was the way he made me feel about myself. Like I wasn't a freak or a loser. Like I was special and smart and beautiful. Like he truly saw me, heard me and understood me.

It was this one-on-one time with him I craved, not his over-the-top attention-seeking behavior around others, or his cruel impatience with people over whom he had power— servers, his staff, his son. I didn't even like him around other people. I wanted him all to myself, as my confidant, my advisor, my mentor, my friend.

Yup, I had fallen in love with my therapist.

As our relationship grew more serious, Ivy amped up her efforts to break us up. She wrote me a rambling, seven-page letter and mailed it in a hand-addressed manila envelope to my office. The gist was that Pazzo was an *awful* person and that she wanted to save me from making a *terrible mistake*. She detailed a side of him I had only caught glimpses of and suggested I ask Angela, his first wife, because she and Ivy were in touch and Angela could confirm everything Ivy was saying.

Then there was a whole section about his coming on to her when he came to pick up Marco. I was physically repulsed as I read it, not wanting to go on but unable to stop.

Ivy described Pazzo's letting himself into her house—he asserted that she never locked her doors—and rubbing his erect penis against her face while she slept. I think I baby-vommed in my mouth as I read it, and yet he did have this gross habit of pressing his erection against my feet while he was standing at the foot of the bed, fully clothed, and I was still sleeping or just waking up. Ivy's assertion didn't seem far-fetched.

Pazzo was rather well-endowed and quite taken with his own manly member. He'd do this disgusting thing when he was naked, maybe just out of the shower, where he'd flop his penis from side to side, slapping his thighs with it, like a truncated elephant's trunk. Anyhow, some things in Ivy's letter rang true.

But I gave the letter to Pazzo, who promptly took it to his lawyer to see if we could get a restraining order against Ivy.

She also called me in the middle of the night, on my

work phone, and left incoherent messages. I remember one in particular in which she played a voicemail from Pazzo. It was hard to hear, but it was definitely his voice, snarling into the phone, but also inexplicably calling her "honey" and "doll," and commenting on her being braless when he came to pick up Marco.

I played it for him when he happened to pop into my office unannounced. I was shaken and felt violated. She was intruding on my work life and messing with my head. He recorded it on his phone to share with his lawyer and then deleted it from my voicemail.

The restraining order hinged on my first telling her that I didn't wish to be contacted anymore, which I did via a letter from Pazzo's lawyer. This was the first step of a cease-and-desist kind of thing. I'm still not clear on all the specifics. Once the court order was granted, Ivy would no longer be able to contact me or come within a certain physical radius. That much was clear. And Pazzo was feeding on the drama like a thirsty vampire.

"She actually *likes* you," he mused, once the legal paperwork was filed. "Thinks she's saving you from a hellish marriage," he laughed with a mischievous glint in his eye, as if this were the funniest thing in the world, a sort of inside joke that he and Ivy and I were all in on.

And I wondered then, as I do now, about Angela Pazzo. The first wife. The *real* wife. And why she and Pazzo had split up. I had so readily accepted his explanation of the heartbreak of infertility.

And why he had abruptly left Detroit and moved to Cherokee Hills. Again, I had accepted without question his story of his lonely one-night stand with Ivy at the Interlochen reunion, in which she had become pregnant with Marco. His burning desire to be a father. His admirable decision to *do the right thing* by her. And then Ivy's ultimate unraveling due to her inherent instability coupled with postpartum depression, conveniently diagnosed by Dr. Pazzo.

Angela Pazzo. Ivy Pazzo. Jennifer Pazzo-to-be. Was there a common thread here? Something I couldn't quite grasp? When these troubling thoughts danced in my head, I didn't *dismiss* them exactly, but I pushed them down and back, like mismatched socks in a drawer.

Red flag.

Narcissists have problems in sustaining satisfying relationships. They can only maintain their facades of normalcy for so long. Eventually they drop the mask and reveal themselves.

And then Ivy went too far in her supposedly well-intentioned efforts to break up Pazzo and me. Super sleuth with too much time on her hands, drinking and smoking and staying up all night googling me, she had stumbled on an actual police mug shot of me. And it was the solid-gold linchpin of her harassment strategy.

Shortly after Pazzo and I had our first date, I went to an industry awards banquet and got stopped on the way home for speeding. I was actually on the phone with my son, negotiating a McDonald's run for him as I drove through a speed-trap on the way home.

20-count McNuggets. Spicy buffalo sauce. Large fries. Oreo McFlurry.

I would later learn from my lawyer that the police hung out in a church parking lot between 10 p.m. and 2 a.m. on Saturday nights because there's something like an 80 percent chance that people have been drinking and driving. This was back in the pre-Uber days. I wasn't usually out that late but had been trying to be a team player, one of the gang, going first to the awards event, where I did indeed have several drinks and then to an afterparty at a downtown club, where I drank only water and danced till I wasn't drunk anymore.

I truly didn't understand that the policeman was going to arrest me and charge me with driving under the influence. He asked if I'd take a breathalyzer test. I refused. He grew belligerent and actually handcuffed me, in my red dress (satin not lace this time) and pearls (not from Pazzo) and threw me in the back of his squad car. I had thought he'd just give me speeding ticket for driving 55 miles per hour in a 40 MPH zone, and I'd be on my way.

But it didn't happen like that. I was put in a paddy wagon with actual bums and drunks rounded up on the street. I was frisked and groped by a female cop at the station and thumb printed—is that even a verb or just a cookie? Although the cop administering the ink pad noted that I didn't have any fingerprints and eyed me suspiciously. I suggested helpfully that I practiced yoga and maybe the tips of my fingers had rubbed off on my mat after years of chaturangas. He looked dubious, convinced I was a hardened criminal who had intentionally erased my identity. I was issued an orange jumpsuit—which incidentally is a terrible color on me—and, after dozing on a hard bench for four hours in a holding cell, they finally took my mug shot. I looked just like Nick Nolte. With braces.

I could go on and on about my night in the Big House and eating prison ravioli with a plastic spork, but suffice it to say it was a humiliating—and sobering—experience that I will never forget. The charges were eventually reduced to speeding. I pled guilty and learned a valuable lesson. And confessed everything to my son and my boss in the interest of penance and full transparency.

Months later, when a co-worker who had mutual Facebook friends with Ivy came into my office and shared Ivy's post with me, I was completely mortified. Ivy had written a lengthy blurb to go with the picture, tagging me in her comments and accusing Pazzo of wanting a degenerate like *me* to be the stepmother of *her* son.

It was impossible for me to believe she had my best interests at heart here. This was not about *saving* me from Pazzo. This was about *destroying* me personally and professionally. She wanted to ruin my reputation and keep Pazzo from gaining full custody of Marco. And not from some maternal instinct either, because she was perfectly content for me to mother Marco, wash his clothes, take him to the dentist, the pediatrician, the optometrist, soothe his nightly nightmares, and dutifully packing his backpack every morning. But Ivy's child support was at stake. And she lived on that.

My private self died a little inside as I was dragged by the hair into the drama vortex that was Pazzo and Ivy's relationship. They would stop at nothing to destroy each other. They used their own son as a ping pong ball—so why wouldn't they use me as an unwitting club to bludgeon each other over the head?

Pazzo's lawyer was able to get the restraining order against Ivy. The Facebook post was eventually removed. But not before it went viral, at least in the shared community of our hometown. Everyone at work saw it. Everyone in my life saw it.

Hell, Nick Nolte probably saw it.

Oddly enough, the effect this sordid incident had on my relationship with Pazzo was to strengthen it. He stood by me, loser girlfriend that I was. I had tumbled off my pedestal and into a bucket of shame. He magnanimously defended me against his psycho ex-wife, with whom I now had no more contact. He had effectively severed the only direct line I had to anyone who really knew my future husband. He had isolated me under the guise of protecting me.

And I fell for it.

I felt lucky to have Pazzo. He made sure to remind me how lucky I was. And now that I no longer had contact with Ivy, the secrets of his past marriages were safely locked away in the vault of her troubled mind. Pazzo had come out smelling like the proverbial rose, or perhaps like the refrigerated FTD bouquets with Baby's Breath he was always sending me.

On our summer visit to Michigan, when we met Papa Alfredo and Neurotic Sister Sophie, Pazzo took me on a side trip to Mackinac Island, a lovely, historic resort located on Lake Huron. We stayed at the Grand Hotel in an elegant suite he had splurged on. There was a bottle of my favorite Veuve Clicquot waiting for us in the room, rose petals sprinkled all around. A view of the street below where horse-drawn carriages clomped by the stately portico lined with benevolent rocking chairs and exuberant geraniums. Pazzo made sure to tell me how much the room cost—causing me to wince—not from the price but from the gaucheness of his desire to reveal it.

Cars aren't allowed on the island, so we took the ferry over and walked around the quaint main street eating fudge and taking pictures. We were happy then, I think. Away from the stress of fighting with Ivy and fretting over Marco, Pazzo was seemingly relaxed and eager to play tourist guide, showing off Michigan's finest to this Tennessee girl.

Pazzo was happiest near the water. An avid sailor, he told me stories of sailing competitions and yacht clubs and regattas, all starring him. I was trying to piece this together with his working-class upbringing in Detroit and black-clad, punk-rocking teen self of the Interlochen era. It seemed there were many phases to Mike Pazzo's life and many faces of Mike Pazzo. He'd seen it all and done it all, and I took him at his word on the sailing thing. He could describe boating knots and was teaching Marco to tie them. My mind wandered when he got into too much detail, but I admired his precision and absolute recall of things, like how to make the perfect Cleat Hitch.

The 1980 film "Somewhere in Time," starring Christopher Reeve and Jane Seymour, was filmed on Mackinac, and there's a cult following now for the flick—special events and people dressed in period clothing gather to marvel at memorabilia and watch the movie over and over again. It tells the story of a man in the 1980s going back in time where he finds his true love. I *wanted* to be in love in this romantic setting.

Back in the room, Pazzo made me put on my favorite red stilettos and do things to him in front of the antique beveled mirror. The whole room was Victorian-era furniture or good reproductions, so my shoes where an anachronism. We'd gone back in time just like Christopher Reeve in the movie. Pazzo liked to watch himself during sex, always performing. He'd take pictures of me too. I couldn't imagine why, since we were together. Why did he need pictures for later? I always covered my face when he did this. I felt disrespected and objectified, but I didn't say no. Afterward, he put the champagne cork in my shoe as a memento.

We ate a lovely meal in the main dining room, where I was already hazy from champagne. Mike never drank to excess. He didn't like to lose control. That was fine with me. I was finding myself drinking more around him and spending most of our time together in a state of mild inebriation. It took the edge off his intense personality and allowed me to overlook his warts and quirks.

After dinner, including the hotel's signature dessert—The Grand Pecan Ball—we meandered to The Terrace Room where a band was playing. Still tipsy from an afternoon of champagne and an evening of wine, I grabbed his hand and playfully dragged him out on the dance floor. I love to dance and grew up with this kind of big band orchestra music at the country club back in Cherokee Hills. I have fond memories of watching my parents dance at debutante balls and weddings over the years.

Pazzo resisted and protested, but I thought he was just being shy. My senses were dulled, and I was feeling carefree and reckless. I fancied myself in love and again had that sense of watching us from the outside, hovering just above the dance floor as the happy couple twirled and swirled, eyes only for each other, a throwback to the love stories the Grand Hotel had witnessed over the years.

I was snapped out of my schoolgirl fantasy when Pazzo yanked me by the arm and abruptly stalked off the dance floor, taking me with him in his furious wake. I couldn't understand what had happened. I thought we were having fun, getting caught up in the moment. He loved music, right?

He's a musician—no, a sailor—no, a psychologist. I couldn't imagine what was wrong.

He turned to me, his face red with rage, and spat out a mouthful of nasty words.

"How dare you humiliate me like that! I've never been so embarrassed in my life. I can't believe you'd do that to me—" and on and on he went. I can't even remember what he said, only the look on his face, which collapsed in on itself like bruised fruit, and the tone of his voice, which was not his voice at all, but a dark, ugly snarl. There was something sinister about Pazzo in that instant, like he wasn't himself, or at least not the happy-go-lucky, in-love-with-Jennifer self I knew.

Red flag.

Narcissists are vulnerable to shame rather than guilt. They believe they are superhuman, and they rely on their ability to be superior over others. If they were part of a hunter-gatherer society they would be more affected by the fact they may have missed a deer with their bow rather than the fact that their family and tribe will have to go without food. Their vulnerability to shame can be so devastating that it consumes them.

Tears flooded my eyes. My face went hot. He had slapped me with a verbal buggy whip, and it stung. The Jekyll/Hydeness of his behavior was so unexpected.

"I'm sorry," I stammered, not sure what for, but it's my natural response, a Southern female, raised to please and placate.

Where was my fiery inner steel magnolia? My spitfire Scarlet O'Hara alter ego?

I can't say. She was missing during these years with Pazzo. He had muzzled me somehow, beaten me into submission with his Svengali-like combination of adoration and praise, combined with hateful verbal abuse and sexual domination.

His psychological manipulation was brilliantly subtle, and he only revealed himself in glimpses. Just when I thought things were great between us, he'd let his mask slip and before I could sort out my feelings of bewilderment and fright, he'd be back to his old charming self. Later, I'd wonder if it even happened.

"It's all right, gorgeous, let's go to bed now."

Whatever I'd done wrong, he had magnanimously forgiven, and now it was time to mess up the bed and then take pictures of me in the claw-footed bath tub. He had a whole series of bathtub shots of me.

After Mackinac Island, we stopped in Anne Arbor—the Paris of the Midwest, Pazzo called it—he had graduated from the University of Michigan and had happy memories of his time there. Ann Arbor was famous for their cherries. We ate lots of chocolate-covered cherries as he led me to his favorite haunts and regaled me with tales of all his friends and the fun they had together there.

Then we went back to Detroit and visited Motown which was actually pretty cool. It was intoxicating to stand in the tiny basement studio where Diana Ross and the Supremes, Smokey Robinson, and so many other legends had recorded. I got caught up in Pazzo the musician and his gigs and his songs and his collection of expensive guitars named after famous female singers like Amy Winehouse. His guitars were always female, and his songs were always written for female voices. When I questioned why he didn't write his own songs and tell his own story, he told me he understood the female perspective from all his years in clinical practice in Michigan. According to Pazzo, his patients had given him a rare and unique glimpse into the female psyche, and it was *their* words he wrote and *their* stories he told.

I thought it was kind of arrogant of a man to think he could tell women's stories, especially a man as domineering and macho as Pazzo. And the lyrics were trite. All the songs sounded alike to me. I much preferred when his band did a rare cover of another artist's music, such as the upbeat adaptation of Steppenwolf's "Born to be Wild" that Pazzo arranged.

But I was impressed with his knowledge of musicology.

He would happily lecture me for hours on music theory and history. And he was deeply influenced by the Blues, which, despite his sense of superiority to all things Southern, were undeniably rooted in the South. Pazzo would speak reverently of what he called the "Holy Trinity of Blues"—Howlin' Wolf, Muddy Waters and B.B. King.

Pazzo had this tattooed, pierced, flame-haired chanteuse with the stage name of "Roxie" in his band. I think her real name was Karen. It was for her that he wrote all his songs. He denied that she was his muse, but she was. A hairdresser by day and singer by night, she fronted for several groups in Nashville, where Pazzo's band was based. Because of his consulting work there once a week, he'd have band rehearsals after work and drive home late. It was Wednesdays, because I taught yoga those nights, so we both did our own thing. It wasn't an issue until we got married, and he expected me to stay home with Marco while he went to Nashville.

In fact, it would fall to me to not only babysit Marco during band practice, but to promote his band and schedule a local benefit concert, generate media coverage and bring a crowd. All of which I did.

But that first summer together, we were still enjoying our romance—we went to Tybee Island together and he spun me around in the ocean till I laughed out loud and felt like a mermaid frolicking in the waves, but safely tethered to this man, who would *protect me and take care of me, wrap me in his love and hold me forever.*

This was after our trip to Mackinac Island. I loved the beach. Was happiest near the ocean. Pazzo wasn't much of a fan, but he humored me then, walking miles every morning along the sand, picking up shells. He'd cower under a sunbrella, covered in zinc oxide while I sunbathed beside him, all greased up with Hawaiian Tropic, content as a cat. The ocean soothed me, the rhythm of the tides, the crashing of the waves. It was a tonic to my soul. While Pazzo was the one who claimed to always hear music in everything, I heard the siren's song of the sea, or maybe it was whales calling, or playful dolphins sending me sonic underwater smiles.

When we left Tybee, Pazzo surprised me with a lovely aquamarine pendant on a delicate silver chain. "It's a drop of ocean water, captured forever for my mermaid to wear when she's away from the sea."

When Pazzo had Marco, we'd do kid-friendly things, although Marco was fretful and hard to please, prone to throwing fits in restaurants and sobbing like a baby in public. His behavior was clearly not age appropriate, but Pazzo had no frame of reference. I was troubled by Marco's obvious impairments and Pazzo's seeming obliviousness to them. He was a psychologist after all. Couldn't he see how Marco struggled? Having already been forced to repeat kindergarten,

Marco had problems at school interacting with other kids and keeping up in class. He couldn't tie his shoes or even zip his pants without help. He often wore his clothes inside out and put on two different sneakers. His gait was peculiar, toes turned out and weight forward on the balls of his feet, as though he were leaning into a stiff wind.

Or else he would mimic his father's stance, placing his palm on his lower back and leaning back into it. Pazzo would sometimes stand like this, as you may recall from our Raccoon Caverns excursion. Marco took it a step further and walked like this, with his hand awkwardly held to his hip, as if it were attached with Velcro.

Foods were either too hot or too cold for Marco. A bee buzzing around our table on a restaurant patio would send him into a paroxysm of fear. He put his hands over his ears when we went to the movies because the music was too loud. Pazzo made him stop, forcibly tearing Marco's hands away from his head. Told him he was just trying to get attention.

Marco was broken in some intangible way. It was as though he were walking around with his skin inside out and all his nerve endings exposed. His heightened sensitivity was almost a superpower, but only for negative sensations. He felt pain more exquisitely than others. His panic was palpable. He was keenly attuned to being hurt.

I never saw it work the other way quite to the same degree— although Marco did love the feel of his special blanket against his cheek, the soft one with teddy bears on it and the silky, hand-stitched binding. He could stand in a hot, steamy shower and lose all track of time, startled back to reality only when the hot water turned to ice. Marco was capable of feeling intense pleasure. "A sensualist," Pazzo called him.

He loved to dance, this peculiar little lost boy. Pazzo had told me the story of Antony Hodgkinson, aka "Dancing Tony," the British drummer who danced convulsively onstage with Nirvana.

"It was like falling; there was no way of stopping it. You just had to go with it. It set the hairs on the back of your neck," Hodgkinson said later in an interview. "You could feel the vibe, the electricity coming off the audience."

Marco lived like that, pogo-ing through life. And when he danced, whether it was in his bedroom or in the middle of a restaurant, much to his father's horror, Marco was entirely himself, enveloped in a warm blanket of sound, surrendering to the music, flapping and flailing with wild abandon.

But mostly, Marco suffered. He was an alien in his own world.

He stood too close to people and laughed too loudly or shut down completely and went into his cocoon, happily building elaborate Lego constructions for hours in his bedroom. He subsisted on cookies and apple juice but couldn't seem to brush his teeth properly, so they were always wearing little sugary fur coats with shiny buttons of plaque. He repeatedly lost his glasses or left them at his mom's when he returned home in too-tiny clothes with no underwear, having left all of his new clothes at Ivy's.

Marco marched to the beat of his own drummer. But he was out of step with the rest of the world.

I remember our first weekend away together with Marco. It was fall now, I was wearing my diamond solitaire on my left hand because it just looked better there. My son was playing soccer and enjoying his senior year in high school, not much interested in my dating life. He'd met both Pazzo and Marco, liked Pazzo well enough and felt sorry for Marco.

The leaves were changing colors, and the heavy humidity had lifted. I was eager to get outdoors and enjoy the singular pleasure of a Southern autumn. I booked a bike trip to The Virginia Creeper Trail in southwestern Virginia. This converted railroad trail between Abingdon and Whitetop, Virginia was something I'd always wanted to do with my own son. In fact, I invited him along, but he demurred. Did I mention that Pazzo used to race bikes professionally? So, he was an accomplished biker and said Marco also enjoyed biking. I hadn't been on a bike since middle school, except maybe at the beach a time or two when my Mike was little, but I was game. It seemed like the perfect outing for our fledgling family-to-be.

Pazzo, Marco, and I set out for the Martha Washington Inn in Abingdon, a historic hotel across from the Barter Theatre, where we'd bought tickets to some kid-friendly play as part of our little adventure.

When we got to the hotel, Marco immediately wanted to check out the pool.

"He's a big swimmer," Pazzo had assured me. "Loves the water. Sometimes we go stay at hotels for the weekend just so Marco can swim in the indoor pools."

I liked the sound of this. My son had swum for 13 years on the summer swim team and was an accomplished swimmer. He had even swum a year on his high school team before deciding to focus on soccer. I started him on swim lessons when he was small. By age six, he and his friends were swimming laps like little porpoises, part of a club program that nurtured young swimmers. He was proficient in all four strokes—including butterfly—and could dive off the starting blocks by the time he was in first grade. I too had swum on the swim team growing up and still enjoyed swimming laps when I had the chance. I considered swimming a lifetime sport and a necessity for safety reasons for pool parties and the beach, which were a big part of my son's childhood and my own.

Marco hated the beach and the sun and the sand, but he did like indoor pools.

I grabbed a glass of wine from the hotel bar and headed out to the steamy terrarium that housed the indoor salt-water pool. There were some other kids in the water, with those noodle floats, splashing about. They looked to be about Marco's age—10-ish or so—that age when little boys have mini biceps and flat bellies, sleek like otters and frisky as puppies. No longer children but not quite teens. On the cusp of adolescence but still Peter Pan-ish in their ability to lose themselves in their games.

I remembered my own beautiful boy at that age and what a joy it was to watch him and his friends together in the water, playing shark or Marco Polo or squirting each other with a vast array of water guns. My Mike had also enjoyed diving for pennies on the bottom of the pool when he was little. He never tired of it, staying in the water till his fingers puckered and his toes bled from scraping the bottom of the pool.

Pazzo and Marco headed up to the room so Marco could change into his trunks.

I was fishing in my purse for pennies to toss into the water when Pazzo arrived with Marco in full-on aquatic regalia. He wore flippers, a diving mask with a built-in snorkel and a swim shirt and trunks, so every inch of his torso was covered. He was sporting inflatable water wings on his arms—you know, the kind diaper-clad toddlers wear in baby pools.

I was taken aback, assuming since we were indoors and not on a deep-sea diving expedition that Marco would simply don a swimsuit and dive in. All I could see of him were his pale arms and shins, like the ghost of a boy, an unearthly creature, oddly out of place. Marco was tall for his age—as I've said before, built like his mother—so he looked older than he was, maybe 12-ish, making his attire even more disconcerting.

The other boys looked up at Marco and grew silent, trying to decide what to make of him. I held my breath for a split second, afraid they would laugh out loud at this peculiar fish out of water. Fortunately, the boys decided to ignore Marco and went on with their games.

Marco struggled slowly into the water, lowering himself an inch at a time, holding a noodle under his armpits. It was painful to watch. I glanced at Pazzo, who looked on fondly, apparently unaware of how out of step his son was with the other boys his age.

I was mortified on Marco's behalf and whispered to Pazzo, "What's with the water wings? I thought you said he could swim?"

"He can. He's just cautious. Those make him feel more secure."

"Good boy, Marco!" he yelled encouragingly at his son, who was now floating on the noodle and kicking with his flippers like an ungainly platypus.

"But can he swim without flotation devices? Can he even put his face in the water?" I persisted.

It seemed urgent to me to strip Marco of his ludicrous costume and normalize him before the other children began to make fun of him. He was bullied at school, and now I could see why. His otherness was palpable. In fact, he'd started seeing the school counselor, initially unbeknownst to Pazzo, who was very angry when the principal refused to share the content of those confidential conversations with him. Student-teacher privilege or some such. Pazzo rationalized Marco's desire to confide in the counselor, saying he was likely troubled by his parents' contentious divorce and Ivy's neglectful mothering.

Now Pazzo seemed to register the other boys and did a quick comparison. His eyes narrowed and his head tilted slightly to one side. Then he put his hand on his low back and puffed out his chest.

"Marco, take off your mask," he commanded, his voice growing deeper and darker.

"But why, Dad? I like it," Marco whined.

"Take it off this instant," his father commanded, escalating the situation past uncomfortable to truly awkward. "Give it to me now."

Marco paddled awkwardly over to the side, with his lipstick-red lower lip protruding and reluctantly handed over the mask. Morbidly fascinated and unable to look away, I piled on and made it worse.

"Marco, can you put your face in the water and blow bubbles?"

"Of course, he can," said Pazzo in that ugly voice I was beginning to recognize with increasing familiarity.

"Marco, swim," he commanded. "Show Jennifer how you can swim."

The other boys were now all watching the spectacle as was their father from across the pool.

Marco dog-paddled lamely in the shallow end, still leaning hard on the noodle, then stood up and looked hopefully back at his father.

"I'll get him swim lessons," I whispered to Pazzo. "No worries, he just hasn't had the opportunity to learn," I added helpfully, knowing that would give Pazzo the opportunity to blame Ivy for being a lousy mother and not teaching her child how to swim. I was hoping to avoid a scene in which Pazzo screamed at his son and berated him until Marco broke down into a puddle of sobs. I'd seen it too many times already. I'd gone into damage-control mode without even realizing it. Fortunately, Pazzo decided not to escalate the situation. He sighed audibly and his eyes grew sad and tired.

"Time to get out now, Marco," said Pazzo. "Let's go."

The next morning was crisp and deliciously clear as we caught the shuttle from the hotel to the top of the trailhead. We'd already decided to do just half of the 35-mile trail, mostly downhill, where we'd meet the shuttle to go back to the hotel. Marco was clutching his bike helmet. It was neon green with a plastic ridge of fringe on the top like Marvin the Martian.

The child had very specific and fanciful tastes that made him stand out even more than he already did. I thought he was too old for a costume bike helmet but kept this thought to myself. Ivy, the artsy one, indulged his differentness and wore it like a badge of honor, not so much to support Marco but to make him into an intentional outcast, just as she had been in high school, a rebel who cut classes and smoked weed, because that's what artists did. Her child was special, and she was special and to hell with the rest of the world. She was daring Pazzo to challenge her.

After Interlochen, Ivy briefly attended Rhode Island School of Design until the money ran out, and she was forced to finish her fine arts degree at the less-prestigious liberal arts college back home in East Tennessee. But she never lost her elitist aesthetic or her scorn for the ordinary, dull lives of conformists.

Then came the fitting of the bikes. There were experts to do it and all sorts of different sizes of bikes. Pazzo, of course, was showing off his superior bike expertise and adjusting the seat of his bike himself. *Where did he get those tools? I wondered. Did he actually bring them with him?*

Meanwhile, Marco wanted a tiny bike that looked like it should have training wheels and streamers on the handle bars. I had taken Mike at his word that Marco could ride a bike, but now I was having my doubts.

"No, no, Marco, that's too small for you," Pazzo barked, taking charge of the situation and picking out a much larger bike. "He's recently been riding a new bike and is still getting used to it," he offered by way of explanation to the bike outfitters.

"But I want the little one," said Marco. "I don't feel *comfortable* on the larger one," emphasizing the school counselor's word he was fond of using. He had told us that she said he should use his words if he didn't feel *comfortable* in a situation.

"Get. On. The. Bike." Mike growled at his son through gritted Chiclet teeth.

With that Pazzo was off, leading the way over rocks and leaves to the trailhead, without a backward glance at Marco. I thought this was some sort of tough-love test, and I actually applauded it. He'd been babying Marco and coddling him—infantilizing him even, to perpetuate his fantasy of being super-dad. It was time for Marco to cowboy up.

I thought of my own son, who had rarely cried even as a toddler. He was stoic and brave and all boy, not this whiny mess of spoiled brattiness that was Marco. And I'll own this, too, I was embarrassed that people would think Marco was *my* son. I'm not proud to admit that, but it's true. Everywhere we went now, people assumed I was his mother and I wasn't *comfortable* with that.

"Not everyone can be perfect, like *Mike*," Pazzo had snarled about my son before, spitting his name out like a bad taste in his mouth. "Just because he's good at everything and handsome and smart." It was clear he resented Mike's normalness and was bitter about Marco's otherness. I found it odd that he commented on Mike's handsomeness, which he often did.

Pazzo didn't look back, and neither did I for a few yards, until it was apparent that Marco was not behind us. It became clear, because he was wailing like a motherless calf at the top of the trail, having walked his bike a few yards, paralyzed with fear, unable to get on the bike. His abject terror was beyond the situation at hand. He was literally freaking out. Hyperventilating. Rocking back and forth. A crowd was gathering. Pazzo sighed and spun his bike around to tend to his son. He tried yelling at him some more and when that didn't have the desired effect, he softened his tone.

Finally, Marco, seeing that we weren't going back, and the van had left, and all the other bikers had whizzed down the trail, got on his bike and rode unsteadily toward me. And miracle of miracles, he got the hang of it. As the trail leveled off, and we got to the little wooden bridges, he even pedaled on ahead, his bright green helmet bobbing in front of us. I said a little prayer of gratitude for the wondrous turn of events, and we made it to the halfway point where The Creeper Trail Café in Damascus serves "the world's best chocolate cake."

We were saved again by sugar. Father and son and step-mother-to-be happily gorging ourselves on cake. And I marveled at the resiliency of children, even peculiar ones, to reach for happiness like a tenuous lifeline and cling to it, with or without water wings.

In his lore about Ivy's mothering mistakes, Pazzo returned to one story again and again. It seems that Ivy, in her hippie-free-spirited way, had taken Marco as a wee toddler, maybe even just a babe in arms, to some outdoor music festival. Her camping equipment was woefully inadequate, and the little tent she pitched blew away in a storm. Marco was left crying piteously in the rain, while his mother was passed out drunk and high beside him. Some well-meaning fellow festival-goers rescued Marco and somehow contacted Pazzo who rushed to save his son, whom he found clutching the chest of a good Samaritan like an orphaned koala bear, reluctant to leave the stranger's arms even to go to his own father, so traumatized was he. And ever since then, Marco has had a crippling fear of thunder and lightning and rain and dark, and this explained why he was always so anxious and couldn't sleep at night. The End.

Because Marco didn't sleep. Ever. Except in class. And at the dinner table. Or in front of the TV lying in the lap of some nurturing babysitter. This insomnia would become my nightmare as well after Pazzo and I were married and I was handed his child to raise. It was like trying to foster a dog that had been chained up and abused. There was no erasing whatever was wrong with Marco, whether it was due to nature, nurture, or neglect. I mistakenly thought I could love him back together again, make him whole, because I was good at mothering, having raised my beautiful boy all by myself. Because, in addition to being a pleaser, I'm a fixer. Or so I thought.

But that night we spent at the Martha Washington Inn, after swimming in the pool and dinner and before biking and eating cake, Marco slept like a lamb. On a cot at the foot of our bed, so we could all stay in the same room. And I had been hopeful that this momentary peace was a preview of our life together.

That first Christmastime with Pazzo was sweet. Marco must have been with Ivy, or rather Ivy's parents—he was close to his maternal grandfather, whom he inexplicably called *Abuelo* although Ivy's family had not a drop of Latino blood in them. Ivy's maiden name was Allen, which was also Marco's middle name. *Abuelo* felt like an affectation, something Pazzo and Ivy thought up to make Marco seem worldly and exotic instead of just a boy born in East Tennessee to a mother of Scots-Irish descent. And wasn't the Sicilian connection exotic enough?

Pazzo had strung Christmas lights over his barren hearth. His house was still in shambles, although I'd bought him a comfy, overstuffed leather club chair for his bedroom. Tried to pull things together a bit, so it felt calm and restful and not like the house had just been ransacked by burglars looking for drugs. There was a huge pool table in the family room—a gift to Ivy from Pazzo—that she had not taken with her when she moved out. Pazzo used it to fold laundry on.

He had wrapped several presents for me and chilled a bottle of wine. We sat in front of the empty fireplace I had filled with lit candles and exchanged our gifts. I don't even remember now what I got for him. Just the Charlie Brown feel of the sad strand of colored lights in the big dark den.

I had recently told Pazzo about a business trip planned with a client to the Turks and Caicos Islands. I'd been to Cabo with the same client, who took his best dealers and customers on an annual junket to some exotic locale. I was invited along because I was fun, so I only had to pay my airfare. I guess they got a block of rooms at the resort, and there were discounts and such.

For one of my Christmas gifts, Pazzo had put sand and seashells and little plastic palm trees in an empty baby food jar with water, making a beach-themed snow globe and explaining that he would pay my airfare and join me on the trip. I was delighted with his creativity and the thought of getting away together, without the constant Ivy phone calls and Marco issues, although I was a little surprised Pazzo would leave his practice, since, as he often pointed out, if he wasn't working, he wasn't billing. He complained about alimony and child support and carrying Ivy's mortgage on the house she had moved into across town, a fixer-upper in an old neighborhood that she planned to flip for a profit.

"Why would your name be on her new mortgage?" I asked, incredulously. "You said she's terrible with money and never pays her bills. Aren't you worried about this affecting your credit?"

"She couldn't qualify unless I co-signed," he replied. "And I have a portion of her alimony diverted directly to the mortgage company, because she can't remember to make the payments, and besides, she'd spend the money on something else."

"So, you own the house then?"

"No, the deed is in her name."

"Your name is on the loan but not on the deed? So, if she defaults it's on you, but if she sells the house, you don't get any of the proceeds? Not even to pay off the balance of the mortgage?"

I was flabbergasted by the stupidity of this. Who would do that? Hold the loan for a house they didn't even own? Obviously, Ivy's divorce lawyer had been better than Pazzo's. He'd been had, but he wouldn't make that mistake again. He'd told me before how Ivy took out a $50,000 cash advance on his credit card to pay for her high-powered attorney. Apparently, that was also being deducted from her alimony payments.

Having been destroyed financially by my first husband's debts, I was scrupulous about these matters. I do have an MBA in finance, but this is pretty basic stuff. Yet Pazzo seemed confused by my queries and unable to grasp the financial implications of his arrangement with Ivy. Could it be that business acumen was lacking in his otherwise flawless intellectual repertoire? In typical Pazzo fashion, he brushed off my questions, and we went back to our little Christmas party, but it seemed to me that he had made some poor financial decisions that would come back to haunt him—and us—later.

But first we were bound for Grand Turk—a midwinter

getaway to an all-inclusive resort—and since Pazzo claimed to *love* to travel, I was eager to travel with him. I'd told him I didn't care so much about *things* but wanted to have *experiences* and if I had time and money I'd like to see as much of the world as possible. I'd been an au pair in France after college and was forever transformed by the experience. My first husband and I had traveled quite a bit before Mike was born, but I hadn't been able to get away much in the years since due to work, my son, and my modest resources.

Last summer's road trips to Michigan and Tybee Island had been delightful experiences, if you overlooked the brief flashes of narcissistic awfulness.

What Pazzo never mentioned was that he is deathly afraid of flying. This didn't sync with the cosmopolitan intellectual jet-setter image he'd cultivated, what with living in London and globetrotting with his colorful Interlochen chums, several of whom had become famous actors, writers, and musicians. One of them was friends with George Clooney and was currently staying in Clooney's house on Lake Como, according to Pazzo.

He told me he had Xanax for the flight, just to help him relax, but the minute the doors locked, Pazzo went into a full-on panic attack. He was panting and gasping for breath. The flight attendants were already strapped into their seats and ready for takeoff when he decided he had to have a glass of water. It all seemed surreal to me, like he was faking it or something. The timing of his distress synced up with maximum attention-getting from all the other passengers. I offered him the water bottle I had carried on the flight with me—but *Nooo*, he needed the attention of a flight attendant *immediately*.

I'll admit I was mortified. After all, I am my mother's daughter, and I don't like drawing attention to myself, especially in public. Besides, I was a guest of my client. Pazzo was sort of a tag-a-long addition to the trip, and now he was making a spectacle of himself. I felt strangely detached as I watched his histrionics. He had told me before that he had a fainting spell in the grocery store when Marco was small and that he had an irregular heartbeat. He was overweight and sleep deprived. I practiced yoga, watched my weight and got as much sleep as I could. It felt like his health issues were self-inflicted and that he was a bit of a hypochondriac. Remember when I had to have stitches, and it was all about him?

Anyway, he eventually calmed down but proved himself to be a high-maintenance traveler. He didn't like to walk on the beach and got winded fast. He refused to take his shirt off in the sun. Wore a tiny biker's hat—due to his elite biking pedigree—instead of a wide-brimmed fedora or Panama hat, so his jowls, neck fat and ears burned to a crisp—for an Italian, he was surprisingly pink, perhaps inheriting his coloring from the land of Lorna Doone. I was reminiscing about our time together on Tybee Island only last summer. Had he only been pretending to enjoy himself? What had changed so much in only a few months?

I'm not gonna lie, I was pretty fit back then and was rocking tiny bikinis and feeling good about it. Pazzo immediately became proprietary about my body and asked me to cover up whenever anyone else was around, which didn't stop him from taking pictures of me naked in the huge jacuzzi tub back in our room. It was like I was his private property, and he tried to shame me for "putting myself on display." He was extremely possessive and became surly when I talked to other men, although he enjoyed catching other women in his enigmatic web of charm, laughing his high-pitched giggle, and gently touching their forearms as he gazed deeply into their eyes—boring a hole right through to their souls. I wasn't jealous. These were older ladies, married for the most part. I was grateful he was interacting with our contingent since we had several client dinners and activities to attend. And it was fascinating to see him seduce and beguile people. I marveled at his mad skills, while realizing that he had bamboozled me as well.

It's like I could watch him snake charm other people yet still be susceptible to his potent powers myself. I know it makes no sense. If he weren't an avowed atheist, I'd say I was under his spell, but that would involve spirits and other-worldly beings and higher powers, right? Pazzo only believed in his own power. He was angel and demon, answering to no one but himself.

The other thing that stands out about the trip was when we were at the airport getting ready to depart. I was happily wandering in the duty free, browsing for rum and vanilla, seeking souvenirs for friends and family. I needed to take some little goodies to my staff.

Pazzo began to panic about missing the flight. We had to get on a bus and go to a different terminal or something. I don't remember exactly. I had passed most of the trip in a lovely rum-induced haze from poolside cocktails served by friendly cabana boys and girls. I found that it helped to drink around Pazzo, to see him through booze-colored glasses, which cast him in the best light. Alcohol had become my Pazzo panacea. I was comfortably numb.

He finally became so impatient that he left me to scout out the bus, and I continued to browse. He didn't come back, and I finally followed the crowd moving in the general direction of our gate. When I walked out onto the tarmac, laden with duty-free bags, he was leaning out of the bus, florid and fuming, and motioning for me to come on, *come on!* He was sweating profusely and waving his arms like a traffic lady at a school crossing. Rather than being flattered at his concern, I was put off. He was always so *Over-The-Top.* Why couldn't he just relax? I wasn't the last one of our group to board the bus. Everything was fine.

There were a few eye rolls from my client and our group—we'd all become buddies during the trip, and some of them I knew from our previous trip to Cabo, when I'd brought my easygoing yoga boyfriend along.

"He was really worried about you," whispered Libby, a veteran of 30-some-odd client trips, who carefully planned the itineraries and ensured that everybody had a great time. She winked at me conspiratorially. Later, after my brief marriage to Pazzo had gone up in flames, she said she and her husband had never liked Pazzo, that he was "bad news" and they had seen right through him. They insisted on meeting any future boyfriends before I married another Pazzo.

He wouldn't speak to me the rest of the trip. Not on the short bus ride and not when we boarded the plane, when he shoved past everyone in line to get on—not even noticing what he was doing. He was in survival mode and was completely unaware of the existence of our fellow passengers, waiting patiently in line to board. And again, I felt responsible for him somehow, like his bad behavior reflected on me, since he was my *plus-one.*

It's worth noting, that even though he thought the bus was leaving me, he didn't come back for me or risk missing the flight to stay with me. It was as though we were on the last chopper out of Saigon rather than a chartered flight from an all-inclusive resort.

Red flag. Red flag.

It was spring now, and Pazzo and I had been dating for over a year. He took to dropping by my office unexpectedly, just to pop in. He cultivated friendships with my staff that didn't include me. One of my favorite employees had been a student of mine when I was an adjunct instructor at our local college. I'd hired Chase after he graduated and considered him a friend as well as a protégé. He mentioned to Pazzo that he'd like to learn to play the drums, so Pazzo began inviting him over to jam in his basement.

Although Pazzo's band was in Nashville and they still practiced and gigged there, he, of course, had a complete drum set and a myriad of guitars at his Cherokee Hills house. He aspired for Marco to become a drummer, so that he would be popular and indispensable to a band.

"Rehearsals are always at the drummer's house," Pazzo explained, "so it's hard to kick a drummer out of your band."

Without acknowledging it, he was already making contingency plans against Marco's future ostracization.

Chase jammed with Pazzo a couple of times. They had a beer or two together. But Chase had his own life, his own friends. Sometimes he canceled on Pazzo at the last minute or didn't show up at all. Hell, he was 24 years old to Pazzo's 50-something. He was just a kid, a typical millennial. He showed up for work and did a great job. That's what mattered to me. Not whether he was being a good friend to my needy boyfriend. I didn't like the way Pazzo was blurring the lines and imposing himself on my work world. I liked a certain separation of personal and professional life. And I needed friends and interests of my own. Pazzo was suffocating me.

Pazzo began to grumble about Chase's irresponsibility and ingratitude for all he, Pazzo, had done for him. Somehow, I was caught in the middle of this and it was *my* fault when Chase didn't keep his end of some imaginary bargain. Because with Pazzo, relationships were transactional. There was *always* an implicit quid pro quo. And Pazzo kept score.

It was exhausting, and I refused to come down on Chase about what he did or didn't do outside the office. It was awkward the way Pazzo insisted on inserting himself into every aspect of my life. I mentioned wanting a mini-refrigerator for my office, so my team and I could keep wine and beer in it for our Friday afternoon meetings. So Pazzo ordered some vintage-looking fridge and a matching microwave online—too expensive and special for what I needed—and insisted on bringing them to the office and making a big fuss about it. Since I didn't want the microwave at all, I put it in the communal kitchen instead of in my office so everyone in the agency could use it. Pazzo was livid. I had offended him by disrespecting his pricey gift—which I neither wanted nor requested. He pouted for a while but finally dropped the subject. Chase, always a free spirit, moved to California.

This was about the time my son Mike was graduating from high school. It had been just the two of us for so long, a decade in fact, and I was overcome with all sorts of emotions—pride, happiness, hope for the future and a bittersweet sadness over the loss of my child through this traditional rite of passage. My friends who were moms all understood this. We'd been through seasons of swim meets, soccer matches, awards banquets, sleepovers, and birthday parties, and now graduation loomed—our babies were all grown up. For me, as the mother of an only child, it was a significant season.

Pazzo volunteered to help Mike with some sort of project he had to complete to graduate. Building a table or something. I forgot why. I think it was part of a community service credit for the International Baccalaureate program. Mike would be receiving his IB diploma in addition to his high school diploma, being part of the inaugural IB program at his high school, the only one of its kind in Cherokee Hills.

Mike hadn't grown up with his father around, something I was painfully aware of and felt guilty about. He had loved my boyfriend and his two sons, with whom we'd spent eight happy years, hiking and camping and playing football. Peter's sons were built-in brothers for Mike. Those were good years, but they were over now, and there was no one to help Mike build this table.

Pazzo to the rescue. In addition to being an accomplished guitar player, biker, race car driver, and sailor, Pazzo prided himself on being handy around the house, although he rarely had time to do any home-improvement projects due to the demands of work and music and Marco. In that order. But he had a rotary saw and a work bench in the basement and was proud of his equipment and tools. He and Mike procured the wood and spent a weekend cutting and sawing and building together with Pazzo sending me pictures via text message to document their progress. He made sure Mike and his friend James wore protective glasses so no wood chips or flying bits of sawdust got in their eyes. There wore work gloves and tool belts. It was a DIY fest for the ages. Songs would be sung and stories told about how marvelous this table was. Pazzo was large and in charge and loving it. All hail the prince of woodworking.

So, *blah blah blah*, the table was finished, and Mike and James turned it in. Their teacher was also their soccer coach, and he was satisfied with the table. Mike checked it off his to-do list and went back to preparing for IB exams, finals, soccer tournaments, and senior prom.

Oh, but it wasn't finished. Not in Pazzo's eyes. He demanded that Mike retrieve it from school and bring it back to Pazzo's basement to be sanded and painted. Mike refused. It was turned in. He got credit. Case closed.

Pazzo was not used to being defied. Marco was terrified of him and visibly quaked in his presence. Pazzo could go from cuddly teddy-bear dad to ferocious grizzly-bear dad in an instant, and Marco melted like a snow cone in the face of his father's unpredictable wrath. Mike, not so much. He had appreciated Pazzo's help and thanked him politely. James borrowed his dad's truck, and together they had turned in the project.

Pazzo resisted the urge to lash out at Mike, so he bashed my son to me instead. It turns out he had clocked the hours spent on the project—as if they'd been billable hours—and kept track of the cost of the supplies.

"I spent 27 hours of my valuable time on this project. Do you know what my time is worth?" He barked at me over the phone. "The table isn't finished. It's not perfect, and Mike should be ashamed to turn it in that way."

I offered to reimburse him for the supplies, but he wasn't

having it. I was missing the point. There was a *right* way and a *wrong* way to build a table. There was a life lesson here, and my child was clearly missing it, which in this neurotic neuropsychologist's opinion, showed a lack of character that would manifest itself throughout my son's life unless I made him finish the table. It was the principle of the thing.

My son was brilliant but lazy. I'd noticed this myself. He usually did just enough to get by academically, easily graduating with over a 4.0 average and got a 30 on his ACT on his first try. Could he have scored higher if he'd taken the ACT a second time or bothered with a prep course? Of course he could. But he didn't care that much. This troubled me, but he was 18 now, and there was very little I could do about it. Pazzo believed I should make Mike pay for college, which I believed was none of Pazzo's business.

I didn't tell Mike how upset Pazzo was because I wanted Mike to like him. I knew they would never be close like he and Peter and the boys were, but I didn't want to push my son away. I was hoping to cobble together a replacement family for the two we'd lost with Mike's dad, Steve, and then Peter and his sons. Replacement is too strong of a word. I thought I could have security and be well loved without losing my son. And I didn't anticipate the demands of caring for a special-needs child. *Someone else's* special-needs child, at that.

To bring the focus back to Marco and away from Mike's upcoming graduation—or maybe it was just coincidental—Pazzo started fretting about Marco's public elementary school not being the right fit for Marco. It was my alma mater and Ivy's and my son Mike's as well. A golden little neighborhood school with involved parents and outstanding teachers who clamored for the plum assignment at the little brick schoolhouse with the quaint bell tower. This jewel of a school had motivated, well-behaved students, good resources, and few of the disciplinary problems that plagued the inner-city schools in the system.

But Marco was still floundering and falling behind. He had attended a Montessori school for kindergarten and then repeated kindergarten at public school, but he couldn't keep up academically or socially. He was awkward and friendless, no longer invited to birthday parties or sleepovers, not interested in sports or extracurricular activities, preferring to play alone in his dark room after school, curtains drawn, lost in a fantasy world of Legos and loneliness. And maybe he wasn't even lonely so much as just a loner. He was happiest in his room. His father would try to force play dates and activities on his asocial son, and Marco would tearfully oblige. Something would always go wrong with these encounters, and Marco would be to blame in his father's eyes.

"I was a gregarious, popular kid," Pazzo told me. "I was always the ringleader in the neighborhood and the quarterback of our football games."

This was the first personal reference to football I'd heard from Pazzo. He regularly ridiculed my devotion to college football and my beloved team. I'd point out that I was a third-generation graduate and two-time alumna as well as a sometimes-adjunct instructor at the local college, not to mention the mother of an incoming freshman, since Mike had decided to attend my alma mater. Having grown up in a college town, my son's loyalties were deeply ingrained.

We felt a vested interest in the sports program, especially football, which is sacred in the South.

"You can't say 'we,'" Pazzo would snarl at me when I referred to the team as my own. "You're not a player. You're not on the team."

In fact, he'd often made fun of our Southern allegiance to football. He just didn't see the point. And when I asked him if he cheered for Michigan or Michigan State, having graduated from both schools, he claimed no allegiance to the sports programs of either institution. Remember, he'd also been a professor of psychology at one or both of those schools.

So, this was news to me now, that he had not only played football as a kid but been the quarterback, no less, of the neighborhood pick-up games. It was as though he rewrote his own personal narrative in the moment to suit whatever point he was trying to make. The point here being clear that he was a well-rounded, well-liked kid, not a misfit like Marco.

We discussed private schools for Marco and landed on the oldest, most expensive, and prestigious prep school in the area. I knew someone in admissions and called to set up an interview.

It could be a fresh start for Marco, we reasoned, *in a more structured environment.* He was a bright kid, albeit peculiar, but the school had become less selective over the years, putting tuition above merit in many cases, so I figured his chances of admission were good.

Back in my day, there were families where one sibling got accepted and another didn't. My own brother was accepted only on the condition that he repeat a grade. He refused and went to public school instead. I had wanted Mike to attend a public high school, so he would have more of a real-world experience than the inevitably elitist climate of private school. Besides, I couldn't have afforded to send him there.

But now that private school started in kindergarten, the

prevailing wisdom was it was easier to get your child in lower school and then he could matriculate to middle school and upper school, rather than trying to compete for fewer spaces that opened up to outsiders in later grades. Pazzo wanted to move Marco for his last year of elementary school to set him up for success in middle school, even though our little neighborhood school was the primary feeder school for all the area private schools.

The big day arrived, and Pazzo took Marco to campus for one-on-one interviews and some group activities as well as a tour of his grade's classrooms. I crossed my fingers and hoped for the best. Pazzo had fussed about what Marco would wear, ultimately dressing him in uncomfortable clothes, with a belt and slicked-down hair, like a mini grown-up. With his glasses and braces and the shoelaces he could not keep tied, he looked especially awkward. Marco had worn Velcro straps until Pazzo met me, and I'd insisted on regular laces so he could learn how to tie them, although at 10 years old, he still struggled with this task mastered by most five-year-olds.

I'm not sure exactly what went wrong. Apparently, Marco was very nervous, taking on the weight of his father's anxiety and soaking up like a sponge Pazzo's obvious disappointment in his son. Pazzo berated Marco the entire way there, complaining about his hair and his shoelaces and his general demeanor, offering last-minute advice and pointers on how to ace the interviews. It was as if Marco were applying for a highly competitive post-collegiate job instead of visiting an elementary school. The pressure was too much for a boy who already knew he didn't measure up in his father's eyes.

Marco tried too hard—blurting out things and interrupting other kids—trying to get attention with his affected grown-up manners and ingratiating remarks to the teachers. But he didn't click with the other children. And, bless his heart, Marco wanted so desperately to fit in, not understanding why his comments were just a little off or his laugh just a little loud. He was not able to keep his hands off the other kids or sit still or pay attention. He was a daydreamy kid most of the time, living in his own head and staring off into space, so his forced interactions with others, especially other children, caused him to overcompensate for his own anxiety with inappropriate behaviors. He was prone to spontaneous hugs and back slaps, not understanding about personal boundaries.

You know when your dog is absolutely fine when nobody's there, but then the doorbell rings and he gets overexcited, sniffing people's crotches and peeing on their feet? That's Marco.

Days went by, and we heard nothing from admissions. I think my friend was too embarrassed to call me because she assumed it was a slam dunk and didn't want to report the negative feedback of the evaluating teachers. Pazzo was beside himself, tearing his hair out, calling the school repeatedly, agonizing over the process and demanding answers, repeatedly asking Marco what he did wrong and involving him in our adult conversations, which was something he did a lot, which I didn't agree with.

Finally, he got the call that Marco would not be part of the 5th grade class in the fall but could apply again in 6th grade. Pazzo was crestfallen. His son had been rejected. He simply couldn't fathom it.

I took the opportunity to suggest we have Marco evaluated by a specialist. It was obvious to me—and everyone else except Pazzo—that Marco was impaired. His pediatrician had long wanted to put him on medication for attention deficit disorder but Pazzo had refused. I reasoned with him that we could get occupational and physical therapists to help Marco. Even the swim instructor I had hired for Marco noted his poor muscle tone and lack of coordination, hallmarks of Asperger's kids, which were more frequently born to mothers in their 40s; in fact, she had one herself. So, she was especially dialed into Marco's deficiencies.

"She's just projecting her own son's issues onto Marco," griped Pazzo, refusing to take any of her feedback seriously.

Now it wasn't just me with my *perfect* son, as Pazzo often referred to Mike, saying something was wrong with Marco. Not just the swim instructor, the pediatrician, his teachers, the guidance counselor, and the therapist Marco had been seeing due to the trauma of his parents' divorce. It was the private school admissions committee, an independent third party that turned down Pazzo's open checkbook rather than admit his son.

Pazzo sadly relented in a moment of weakness. I believed in that moment that he truly loved Marco and could put his son's needs above his own ego. I breathed a sigh of relief for Marco and for myself, as I imagined the path ahead getting smoother for both of us. But that's not what happened.

About that time, I got a job offer to move out of town—it was a dream job, as president of a public relations firm in North Carolina. Mike was starting college in the fall, so the timing was actually pretty perfect. I was conflicted about leaving my elderly parents, but they were happy for me. I had been bound to Cherokee Hills earlier in life due to my first husband's job. He was older and already established in his career when we got married. Then I stayed home when Mike was little, savoring every moment and milestone, ultimately working nights in a local call center just so I didn't have to leave him during the day.

As my then-husband's career foundered and his debts mounted, I began to work part time and finally went to work full time when Mike was in second grade, the same year I divorced Mike's dad. Steve had said his debts couldn't touch us personally, but when my wages were garnished to pay his company's back taxes to the IRS, I left him and never looked back. I had to build a future for my son, starting from scratch. And now I would be able to pay for four years of college for him, with no help from Pazzo, and it was finally *my* turn.

Cue the Mary Tyler Moore theme song.

Except Pazzo. He was initially excited for me and claimed he could move his practice from Tennessee to North Carolina just as he had moved it from Michigan to Tennessee. We hadn't set a wedding date yet. Plans were fluid. But this was a big decision that affected us both.

"But what about Marco?" I asked, knowing Ivy would never let him move across state lines with his son.

"Oh, it's okay; our lawyers can work it out. Ivy's crazy, but deep down she wants what's best for Marco."

I pushed my own doubts aside and accepted the job. Mike had been wait-listed at Davidson College, so I had vague hopes of moving him to North Carolina with me and paying in-state tuition at Davidson. Wasn't sure how all that worked but was going to look into it.

My new company offered to let me work remotely until Mike went to school in the fall, flying me over for meetings as needed. They were being so accommodating and helpful. It was almost too good to be true. They had a hair salon for a client, so hair appointments were included as a perk in my contract. Also ballet tickets.

I gave my notice at my agency. Put my house on the market. It sold in 48 hours.

I was full steam ahead. Mary Richards at midlife. Starting anew at twice my current salary. *Well it's time you started livin' It's time you let someone else do some giving— you're gonna make it after all!*

Then Pazzo dropped his bombshell. Turns out Ivy hadn't seen things the same way he had. Marco would leave Tennessee over her dead body. Even though Pazzo was the custodial parent, she still had to give permission for him to move their child. I had known this all along. On some level. After all, I was a divorced mother myself. I would never have let Mike's father move him, but it had never come up. I had raised Mike with no financial support and very little parental involvement from Steve. That last part breaks my heart to this day.

I had to renege on the job offer. I'd already given notice at work, but Pazzo said I could start my own company and work from home. He'd pay all our bills and I could focus on building my business. I'd done consulting work before and liked the freedom of it. Maybe I could even freelance for my previous employer. We'd parted on good terms. Maybe this was always what was meant to happen.

And if I'm being honest, I'd been scared about starting over at my age. This felt safe. And I didn't really want to leave Mike, even though he was leaving the nest. I felt like the nest should stay right where he left it with his Mother Bird still in it.

I opted to stay in my comfort zone and then used Pazzo as an excuse for doing it. Instead of running like hell when I had the chance. Once again, I ignored the red flags of his misrepresenting his circumstances to me and reeling me back into our relationship, beginning to isolate me now that I'd no longer be working outside the home. I would have to depend on him for insurance coverage. He would have control of our spending since he made the big bucks.

He'd had no intention of leaving Tennessee. But now he had cut my legs out from under me, and I'd handed him the scythe. I had no house and no job. Just him.

Instead of house hunting in North Carolina, I was house hunting in Cherokee Hills. And Pazzo loomed large in the process. We ended up in a gated community with a big fat mortgage payment I couldn't afford. He assured me he'd take care of it. But he was cash poor at the moment and couldn't get approved for the jumbo loan, since he was already carrying two mortgages on his and Ivy's houses. Like a fool, I wrote the $100,000 check for the down payment with the money I'd been saving for a decade for Mike's college fund. And then, because it was easier for me to get approval, it was my name on the mortgage. Not Pazzo's.

I was carrying all the financial risk. If he didn't make the payments, it was my credit that would be ruined. I'd be financially accountable. Just like in my first marriage. What the hell was I thinking? It was as though momentum was carrying me along now, and there was no turning back. I was riding a wave. Pazzo was pulling me behind his boat, and I couldn't let go of the tow rope. Or wouldn't let go. Because it was easier just to go with the flow.

And since I'd schooled Pazzo on his own stupidity of

not being listed on the deed to Ivy's house, he emphatically insisted on being listed on the deed to *our*—technically *my*—house. I said no to that. So, I wasn't completely steamrolled. We had a prenup that said when he paid back half of the down payment, which he was to do upon the sale of his house, then I would add his name to the deed.

There were two bedrooms beside the master suite in *our* new house. One was closer to the garage and the front door. The other was closer to the bathroom that Marco and Mike would share. I thought the front bedroom made sense for Mike, because he'd be driving and coming and going at late hours and would be less likely to wake light-sleeping, anxious little Marco, who also had tummy issues and needed to visit the bathroom frequently during the night. Marco liked his room at the back of the house. With the shades drawn. Door shut.

But Pazzo wasn't having it. The front bedroom had a larger closet, and Marco needed that since he was giving up an adjacent playroom at his current house and because he had so many toys. Mountains of Legos and model airplanes and remote-controlled cars and kites and a telescope and stuffed animals and hanging models of the solar system and Star Wars memorabilia and every single thing that his father had ever bought him, some of it still in the original boxes.

I suggested culling the collection. World War III ensued.

You see, I'm a bit of a minimalist. Was raised by packrats. My parents were children of the Depression, saving every issue of *National Geographic* because you never know when you might need it. My first husband was much attached to things as well. I'd been clearing clutter all my life. I craved surfaces and order, probably since so much of my life was chaos, it was my way of feeling in control. And, besides, it looked good. All my friends decorated their homes, and their husbands stayed out of it. My first husband had been like that, too. He was grateful that I organized our life.

Sometimes I even make the bed in hotel rooms. What can I say? I'm tidy. So, shoot me.

But Pazzo's identity as super-father was clearly dependent on Marco's massive cache of material possessions. He took perverse pride in letting Marco leave them all over his house in every room. The playroom next to Marco's bedroom was nothing but overflow. Marco didn't even play in there because there was no clear path through the mess.

Again, I've conveniently blocked out how all this was resolved. I think we sent some things to Ivy's and to Abuelo's house and stored a bunch of stuff in the garage. We put shelves in Marco's closet and storage bins under his bed, which I meticulously organized to help him stay on top of all his stuff. He'd never had to clean up after himself, was a tiny tyrant in his father's bachelor castle, and now he seemed to appreciate some order in his chaotic little life. He wanted to put his Legos in bins like they did at school rather than tripping over them with his sensitive Pazzo feet. So, an uneasy truce was reached.

But Pazzo mightily resented that my son got the larger closet. And I was stupidly amazed once again at the smallest things that set him off. I began to walk on eggshells—like walking on Legos—around Pazzo, especially where Marco was concerned. Any perceived inequity between my son and his was unacceptable to Pazzo. Never mind the fact that my son was an adult and Marco was a child, that my son took good care of his few prized possessions and picked up after himself. Pazzo thought the same rules should apply, regardless.

Red flag. Red flag.

I never told Mike about the closet altercation. Because I wanted him to like Pazzo.

I was in no hurry to marry Pazzo. Was having serious reservations. He was increasingly possessive and demanding, surly and unpredictable.

We went out to dinner and I casually referred to him as "baby" in front of the server, as in "Hey baby, what are you hungry for?" It was a term of endearment like sweetie or honey. He called me goddess and insisted on huge PDA in front of everyone, so I didn't think anything about it. This is the South, after all. Every sentence ends in sweetie, honey, baby.

The server took our order, and after she walked away he looked at me coldly and said, "Don't ever humiliate me that way again in public. How *dare* you refer to me as *baby*?"

These mood swings were like storm clouds at the beach. They could appear suddenly out of nowhere and vanish just as quickly, leaving you soaked and shivering in the sunlight.

Pazzo spewed his carefully chosen insults with loathing and disgust. Venom dripped from each syllable. His pitch would go an octave lower, and he would precisely enunciate each word.

It was almost as though he were a split personality or overcome by evil spirits. You know in movies, when the priest is conducting an exorcism and the possessed person starts speaking in a completely different voice? That's what it was like with Pazzo. He became a stranger, and his whole demeanor changed. His voice had a different pitch and cadence. It was some scary shit.

But then when it was over, and he was himself again, you'd think you dreamed it, or that it never happened at all.

Pazzo conducted psychological examinations of people accused of heinous crimes who claimed insanity as a defense for their actions. This was a lucrative side hustle of his. He was a much sought-after expert witness at trials, because he could be paid to say whatever the defense or the prosecution wanted him to say—I only found out about his reputation later.

But something that always stuck with me was Pazzo's description of meeting with murderers, rapists, and psychopaths, and how you could feel a "cool breeze coming off them because they were empty and soulless."

Well, in those moments when Pazzo turned on me and attacked me with his words, I felt that cool breeze wafting off him like devil's breath.

We went to a fundraiser hosted by dear friends of mine. I knew everyone in the room and was hugging and catching up with folks. I introduced Pazzo to people until he grew tired of being my sidekick. He button-holed one person by the bar and hunkered down for an intense one-on-one. I happily flitted around the room, wine glass in hand. These were my people, and I was having fun.

After we left the gathering, Pazzo said, "I'm going to teach you how to *actually* communicate."

I looked at him, puzzled. Had I done something wrong? Did I embarrass myself and not know it? I felt loved and accepted by my old friends and business acquaintances, many of whom had served on the board when I was president of the local chapter of the marketing association. What had I missed?

"You were so shallow and superficial," he spat out the words. "You were just working the room. It was very offensive and off-putting. People were staring at you. You were making a fool of yourself."

When he saw that his barbed words stung, he countered soothingly, "Don't worry. I can teach you how to talk to people in a way that shows you are truly interested in them and that you actually care what they're saying."

"But I *am* interested. I *do* care," I protested weakly.

I'd grown up in a very *social* family, in every sense of the word. My parents *entertained* at home and at our local country club. I'd been *presented to society* in the old-school sense of the term. These notions may seem silly and antiquated now, but they were very much a part of my upbringing. I learned the fine art of conversation at the feet of my father, a silver-tongued, Southern gentleman, quick-witted, kind, and an excellent listener.

Pazzo was a neuropsychologist though. He was trained to pick up on social cues and observe human interactions. Maybe I'd been doing it all wrong all along?

Which begs the question: if I was so terrible to be around, so socially inept, why was he so keen to marry me—so *crazy* about me? Why did he so desperately want me on his arm? Or did he really just want my severed head on his wall, a bloody trophy of his latest female conquest?

I see now that he was threatened, because I was the center of attention in my little group. He didn't know anyone, and it wasn't *about* him, so he sulked in a corner, bending the ear of a trapped listener, a captive audience of one.

Red flag.

With narcissists, there's an obvious self-focus in interpersonal exchanges, often to the extreme.

I'd been brought up to meet and mingle. I worked in public relations. Communication was my job. But Pazzo had a way of finding my vulnerabilities, playing on my insecurities and making me doubt myself. Then he'd cast himself as my savior. He could scan me for weak spots and then insert tiny daggers at will—like acupuncture needles or the pins in a butterfly's head.

I thought I was rebounding nicely from my breakup with Peter, but maybe it was just that—a *rebound* relationship. And maybe Pazzo sensed my doubt not only about myself but about our viability as a couple, so he was subtly changing tactics, from praise and adoration to breaking me down with verbal abuse. The self-doubt and unworthiness I'd felt after my breakup came flooding back, and Pazzo played me perfectly. I began to think I was lucky to have him since I was such a loser, and that maybe he was my last chance at love.

Marriage
&
Unmasking the Monster

I had assumed we could just live together in my new house, but it was then Pazzo told me about the morality clause in his divorce and parenting agreement. He couldn't have anyone spend the night when Marco was around. Unless we were married. Then it would be okay. Interesting timing to mention this, after I'd quit my job and signed a big fat mortgage.

And how was I going to pay this mortgage or even support myself without Pazzo? Suddenly I was dependent on him. *Dammit*. How had I let this happen? If I didn't marry him, I'd be stuck in a house I couldn't afford with no visible means of support. This was no time for second thoughts.

Pazzo had graciously agreed to pay the first month's mortgage, and then we would get married, and then he and Marco would move in. Marco would be with Ivy for Labor Day weekend, so we planned a brief civil ceremony—a flash wedding in a downtown pocket park—performed by my cousin's wife, a retired Unitarian minister. In the end, neither Marco nor Mike was there, Pazzo convincing me that it wasn't fair to have my adult son present at the wedding if his child wasn't there, too.

I bought myself a bouquet at Kroger. Pazzo bought me a Tiffany wedding band and a dress in Atlanta, vetoing the one I chose as being too revealing. It was ivory lace, strapless, and fitted with a flesh-colored lining.

"It looks like you're *naked*," he'd snapped.

I selected a sheath dress instead with a demure scoop neckline and short sleeves.

We wrote our own vows—which Pazzo insisted on memorizing rather than having my cousin prompt us. I dutifully practiced mine and delivered them at the appropriate moment. He completely blanked, his eyes swelling and his face turning crimson. He was sweating through his shirt; the collar was too tight around his thick neck. He'd had a bad haircut the day before, which only accentuated his corpulence. I noticed, without meaning too, that he'd put on weight since we'd been together. He looked like SpongeBob SquarePants in a suit.

"Marriage is a noble estate, revered as the most honorable and tender of human relationships. Enter with reverence and discretion. A true marriage achieves a meaning of the Sanskrit *Namaste*," my cousin said.

"The light in me sees, hears, and understands the light in you."

I'd hired a photographer to take a few candid shots of us, people walking by, a regular Friday morning, with a lovely spontaneous wedding happening among the art installations and hydrangeas at this little urban oasis. My new husband wouldn't look at the camera. Kept feigning romantic moments, burying his sweaty face in my neck or dipping me in an awkward dance move. He was hyperactive and distracted. Melting in his jacket which he finally took off. There are no pictures of him looking forward, only sideways and away from the camera. I told myself it was because he only had eyes for me.

We lunched, just the two of us, at the elegant restaurant where he bought the $50-a-snifter single-malt Scotch—and also where I'd had my first wedding reception, a supper dance upstairs in the ballroom. He knew that. It was like he wanted to write himself into my previous life and erase any memories of anyone else. He'd even asked for my pre-engagement ring back to exchange it for a three-diamond ring, exactly like my first engagement ring. I declined and said I preferred the solitaire.

And yes, he gave me a strand of pearls. I'd even torn some pictures out of magazines showing him the kind of necklace I'd like, maybe freshwater pearls on a leather string, something unique and unconventional. I had drawers full of my mother's and grandmother's traditional cultured pearls, strands of various lengths. Also, from my first husband. They were reminders of a traditional life I'd outgrown, my first marriage as The Perfect Wife. Giving dinner parties and doing Junior League work. A life I'd happily left behind in my forties as a working single mom. Yoga was my moving meditation now. The beach was my spiritual home. I had no interest in going back to being an '80s housewife.

Of course, he bought me a single strand of perfectly matched cultured pearls, big as bath-oil beads. Ladylike and traditional. Very Betty Draper from *Mad Men*. I dutifully wore them on our wedding day.

We celebrated with Veuve Cliquot and then it was off to an elegant mountain resort for our mini-moon. He'd booked a little cabin away from the main hotel, with rose petals and candles. Outdoor hot tub. It was Mackinac Island redux. I drank a lot of champagne. We had a lot of sex. I told myself this was what happiness felt like. Being loved. Being secure and settled.

My parents were pleased—well, my dad was. My mom was never a Pazzo fan. He couldn't win her over no matter how hard he tried. She was cat-like in her affections. Discerning and distant. Mike was happy for me. Although he didn't say much, I knew he had worried about me since the breakup with Peter. Both my son and I mourned the loss of the family we'd built with Peter and his sons. Mike and I still got together with the boys, who even came to visit my parents, referring to them as "G-Mom" and "Doo," just as Mike did, so much a part of our lives had they become.

We got back on Saturday night, the first night we would spend in our new house. Marco's room was all set up, and he was eager to join our new little family. Mike was off somewhere with friends. He'd been coming and going at the house already, since we'd lived there for several weeks, just the two of us. We tucked Marco into his old bed in his new room, carefully painted the exact shade of blue as his old room. As we lay down together as man and wife, I was rolling my new name over on my tongue, "Jennifer Pazzo." I toyed with not changing my name since I had professional equity in my previous married name and had used it for longer than even my maiden name. Fifteen years of marriage and 10 years of being single.

My husband was softly snoring when I heard the moaning and groaning coming from Marco's room.

"Mike, something's wrong," I nudged him. He awoke with a start. He had wanted to keep a baby monitor in our room because Marco was prone to nightmares, but I had nixed this idea. The kid was 11 years old for goodness sake.

We tiptoed into Marco's room to find him holding his belly and complaining of terrible pain. I wanted to give him a hot water bottle and some over-the-counter meds and go back to bed. I suspected it was psychosomatic as he often complained of mysterious stomachaches at school and spent many weekday afternoons in the nurses' office or on his mother's couch playing video games.

But Pazzo was having none of that. "You're just like your mother, callous and unfeeling," he spewed the words at me, almost gleefully. He knew just how to wound me, knew all my childhood secrets, having wormed them out of me early in our relationship. He knew my mother had not been particularly nurturing. He also knew I had been extremely nurturing with my own son, but that Mike was rarely sick and that I generally took a tough-love approach to maladies with no physical evidence.

We were off to the ER, where Pazzo eagerly told the attending physician that Marco had a twisted bowel or some such at birth—the first I'd heard of this—no doubt Ivy's fault for poor prenatal care. Anyway, Marco had a sensitive stomach, and his intestines could rupture and this was really, *really* serious, according to his father. The doctor did his due diligence and pronounced Marco constipated, administered a suppository and sent us home. Marco was much improved by this time, sitting up and chatting with all the nurses, tickled to have his father's undivided attention and everyone else's in the room with his overly precocious little adult talk.

I didn't think he made it up. I thought he really felt it, and I saw now that Marco was fragile, even more fragile than I'd realized. He *felt* everything very deeply, and he was troubled by our marriage, worried about his mom, and unsure of his place in the world. That manifested in the bellyache to end all bellyaches, except it didn't end. Ever.

When Marco didn't get into our first-choice private school, we'd opted for a different one that had a reputation of taking children who didn't get in elsewhere. Problem children with overly protective, hyper-vigilant helicopter parents. Older parents whose too-precious children needed lots of hands-on care. I dutifully bought Marco's uniforms and joined the parent organization. It fell to me to pack his lunches—he didn't like the cafeteria food—and attend his field trips—since I had a flexible schedule now. And, of course, I picked him up after school every day and took him to swim lessons or the orthodontist or on errands with me.

One day I arrived to find the aftercare teacher and a room full of kids but no Marco.

"He's resting in a dark room," explained Miss Tracy.

When she saw my blank expression, she explained that he had forgotten to wear his headphones at the student assembly, and the loud noise had upset him. I had no idea he wore headphones at assemblies. We'd had to purchase them because he couldn't seem to concentrate in class, even after the teacher had put up cardboard partitions between Marco's desk and the students on either side of him. I didn't quite know what to make of this. Maybe my own son *had* been perfect after all.

I took Marco home. He was sullen and silent, ashamed of the whole incident and dreading his father's response.

While he knew it was okay to be *different* at school, it was not okay with Pazzo, who roared at Marco when he heard about what happened.

"You don't need headphones, Marco. You're just doing this to get attention," he said sternly. "I want you to stop it right now."

Marco stared miserably at his plate, poking at the food, not touching the tall glass of milk that I'd made a supper-time staple instead of his beloved juice boxes and Sunny D. The orthodontist had warned that he'd have to take Marco's braces off if the child couldn't do a better job of brushing his teeth and laying off the sugar that was rotting them under the metal bands.

I was trying to parent Marco the way I'd parented Mike. My son had turned out tall and healthy and smart and well-adjusted. He had his issues, but nothing like Marco's crippling psychological afflictions. Between my trying to set boundaries and normalize him and his father's alternating rage and infantilization, Marco was a mess. Then there was Ivy who apparently did no parenting whatsoever. She and Marco were more like naughty children together, staying up all night binging on movies, eating junk food, and going weekends without bathing.

This was my life now. All of a sudden, instead of a new career as president of a PR firm, my son in college, and money in the bank, I was a full-time mother again, for a child that resented me and was, frankly, hard to love. Which I felt terribly guilty about.

We had our sweet moments together—like the time our gentle dog Hank found a hummingbird in the driveway. Our sweet, docile canine was just staring down at the tiny creature struggling to escape a shroud of cobwebs in which it was entangled.

"Look," Marco exclaimed, mesmerized by the fragile bird, its emerald green throat iridescent in the sunlight, its tiny wings, flapping furiously.

As I knelt down and gently picked it up, Marco looked at me with solemnity and said, "We have to save it."

I carefully unwrapped its wings and toothpick-sized bird legs, its itty-bitty beak, which was shut with the sticky material of the dusty cobwebs. I never realized how glue-like the consistency of cobwebs would be. It was as though I was peeling chewed gum off his delicate bird parts and trying not to break him at the same time. See what I did there? I made the bird a *he*.

One of Mike's favorite books as a child was *Are You My Mother?* by P. D. Eastman. It had been a favorite of mine when I was little, too. You'll recall that a bird taps his way out of his shell while his mother is away and wanders around looking everywhere for her.

Maybe my inner under-mothered waif related to the story, usually read aloud to me by my grandmother. Of course, I had a mother, but she was not much present in my life, more like the *whah whah whah* parent sounds in the background of Charlie Brown cartoons. So, some part of me is always saving little birds and broken toys and Mike and Marco...

The hummingbird's fierce little heart was beating right out of his breast, and I feared he would die of fright before I could free him. But finally, I got most of the grey mess off and invited Marco to share this magical moment with me as I placed him in a bush where he could catch his breath and then fly away, hopefully before our predatory puss-in-boots,

Richard Parker, could eat him all up. It felt like a momentous occasion, something Marco and I would secretly share and marvel at forever.

But when it was time to leave the cool shade of the garage and walk across the tall prickly grass in the broiling sun, Marco balked.

"It's too hot," he said simply and went inside to play Minecraft, the video game to which he was currently addicted, having lost interest in our avian rescue project.

My jaw dropped and my heart sank that he would miss out on this special moment. Hank and I made our way across the lawn and reverently placed the bird on a branch in a bush and backed away. When I went out later he was gone. I like to think he took flight and was on his way to north as part of the great migration or perhaps to a nearby hummingbird feeder in a neighbor's yard.

When I went inside to report that Operation Hummingbird was successful, Marco was happily ensconced on the sofa eating Cheetos and watching *Dr. Who* on TV.

Pazzo continued to go to Nashville on Wednesdays. I had to get a babysitter so I could teach my yoga class. I thought 11 was old enough to stay home alone for a couple of hours, but Pazzo wouldn't hear of it. Whereas Mike had gone to bed at 8 o'clock sharp for most of his childhood, Marco never slept. I'd come home from yoga to find him still up. I'd pay the babysitter, clean up all the little messes of snacks and dirty Kleenexes, rogue socks, and scattered schoolwork. Marco would help me when I asked him.

Then we'd struggle through brushing teeth—more difficult

than tying shoes. I had added mouthwash to his oral hygiene routine, but he cringed at the taste, eyes watering, saying it burned his mouth. Finally, we'd get his pajamas on and his room picked up. We'd lay out his clothes for the next day because getting ready in the morning was such a challenge and Pazzo would get angry and impatient if Marco was running late. Ivy never cared and let him sleep in and miss school, so we were constantly undoing the un-routine he had at her house and resetting his schedule at our house. No sooner had I turned out the lights—but not all the lights, because Marco was terrified of the dark—and walked out of his room to do laundry and sit down for a moment with a glass of wine, than I'd hear the quiet whimpering. Marco. Never. Slept. He cried and worried and stayed up all night. Especially when his father was gone.

Then he overslept in the morning, fell asleep at breakfast and in class, and sleepwalked his day through school, inattentive, drowsy, and distracted. He'd fall asleep in the backseat after school, while the car was still in the pickup line. It was a pattern we could not break. Rare was the day I didn't get a call from school to come get him early due to stomachaches. He forgot to write down his homework assignment. He came home with the dreaded pink slips for behavior problems. I couldn't get my work done, much less buy groceries and pick up Pazzo's dry cleaning and check on my parents, who had begun to have falls and strokes and other issues.

Then the parent-teacher conferences started. And the school counselor again. And the isolation from other kids. *Just like before.* It seemed wherever Marco went, he never belonged. His only friends were the school nurse and the kindly teacher's assistant who had to sit with him to calm him down after he threw a tantrum and kicked other kids at recess or burst into tears and crawled under a table at gym class rather than play volleyball.

He was a misfit. It was heartbreaking and frustrating. I couldn't seem to help him, no matter how much I tried. We did make small progress, but it was never good enough for Pazzo, who would end up doing Marco's homework for him rather than have it undone. Marco was brilliant, Pazzo complained. They were just teaching the material the wrong way.

And when the therapist we went to see to have him evaluated pronounced him severely delayed and recommended regular sessions to work with his poor motor skills and the developmental milestones he'd missed along the way because he was clearly impaired, his father was livid.

"She has a vested interest in making that diagnosis. It's like asking a barber if you need a haircut," he sputtered. "I'm not sending Marco somewhere where there are retarded children. It will negatively impact his self-esteem."

Or Pazzo's self-esteem, I thought.

I fought hard for treatment. We were seeing some improvement now at swimming lessons, going twice a week. And Marco was feeling more confident in the water. I reasoned that being able to perform simple tasks like handwriting and teeth-brushing would have the same positive effects. Pazzo finally relented but insisted on home therapy. It wasn't available through this facility, and we never got around to finding another.

Pazzo complained that I had given Marco's pediatrician an unbalanced view of his behavior, hence her recommendation for the evaluation. Pazzo, of course, had been out of town and unable to attend the check-up. But he called later and refuted everything I'd told the doctor, my concerns about Marco and his special needs.

I was just the stepmother. What did I know? Except I took care of Marco full-time now. He only saw Ivy a couple of weekends a month, as Pazzo had used me as evidence of his stable two-parent household and been able to negotiate a decrease in Ivy's child support as an added bonus.

Meanwhile, he still hadn't sold his house due to *deferred maintenance issues*, so he was now making three mortgage payments and working all the billable hours he could. The care and upkeep of his unsold house fell to me, of course. I met with the real estate agents Pazzo hired and fired. Staged the house for showings. Hired a yardman to keep up the two-acre property. Pazzo had allergies and didn't do yardwork, which didn't stop him from complaining about the price and the quality of the work that was done.

I found myself taking care of two households, one of them an old rundown house in my childhood neighborhood, where Pazzo had felt legit. It was a status symbol—the housing equivalent of a Jaguar or a Porsche. But stately old houses take constant maintenance. Built in the '20s, Pazzo's house had structural damage because of water in the basement and gutters he never cleaned and leaks in the skylight in Marco's playroom. Ivy had partially renovated the kitchen but had cut a lot of corners.

Pazzo wanted to get back the $750,000 he had paid for the house when he bought it sight unseen from Michigan at Ivy's insistence. We'd be lucky to get $450,000 as a fixer-upper. After we resolved the asbestos and radon and everything the home inspectors came up with. Contracts fell through, and the house got the reputation on the market as damaged goods. My husband already had a reputation as being difficult to work with. I didn't realize he'd tried to unload it twice already during his marriage to Ivy. I couldn't find a Realtor who would work with him.

And this meant that even if he sold the house, he'd be upside down on the mortgage. There would be no equity to pay me back for his half of the down payment on our home. And half wasn't really fair anyway since he made half a million dollars a year, as he was proud of pointing out. I had made a fraction of that, even when I worked full time. Now I was freelancing and paying for Mike's college. But I had signed the prenup, which only showed his mortgaged assets and didn't reflect the back taxes he owed to the IRS. It was déjà vu all over again, the financial infidelities of my first marriage coming back to haunt me.

Fall and Marco's first semester at private school came to a tearful close. We went to Universal Studios over Christmas to visit Harry Potter World. Marco was too fearful to ride the rides, after waiting in line for hours, to his father's great consternation. They were mostly virtual rides with special 3D glasses where you just sat in an open car that jiggled around and stared at a screen which simulated special effects. We sat in the one for handicapped people that didn't rock and pitch, since the motion seemed to terrify Marco. And the loud noises had him constantly muffling his ears with his hands, much to his father's disgust.

We stopped in St. Augustine on the way home, having driven to Florida, as Pazzo didn't want to fly. We'd scheduled something I'd always wanted to do, an interactive swim with dolphins. It was an outdoor tank, and Marco and I donned wetsuits. Again, he was terrified and resistant to the adventure, preferring the gift shop with stuffed dolphins to the actual experience. But I took him by the hand and we got in the tank with the trainer, who gave us instructions on what to expect and how to interact. Marco was shivering so badly his teeth chattered.

And yet, when the dolphin surfaced and let us touch him, something truly magical happened. Marco became unafraid and was suddenly fully present in that moment. He was miraculously transfixed by the beautiful creature, as was I. It was just us in the tank so we got a lot of time with the large, playful mammal, whose size was slightly intimidating. I'll never forget the smooth texture of its skin as we stroked it. Marco put his face to the dolphin's nose, and they both smiled. And I thought, in that moment, that maybe there was hope for this fragile little boy and that a little kindness could make a world of difference.

Notable in his absence was Pazzo, who was content to stay fully clothed on dry land and take pictures from afar. And make important phone calls. But even he sensed the magic of the moment. And I think he was probably proud of Marco and maybe even happy for him—if narcissists can feel happiness for others. I've never understood the total lack of empathy thing, because I'm too full of empathy for my own good. I need better personal boundaries to other people's pain and suffering.

All I can say is Marco made a connection that day with this marvelous sea mammal, and it was beautiful. It was New Year's Day and anything seemed possible. I wanted to hold onto the specialness, somehow bottle it and bring it home with us to restore our hopes and reimagine my tenuous and turbulent relationship with Pazzo. I bought an ornament painted by a dolphin as a souvenir of our trip. For our happily ever after of future Christmases together.

It was January and my birthday was coming up. After my Paris Birthday Trip, I was looking forward to a quiet celebration, maybe just dinner out with my husband. Guiltily I hoped that Marco would be with Ivy so there would be no tears or tantrums and no tension between him and his father. I wanted my own son to be part of the celebration but knew better than to suggest it, as Pazzo's resentment for Mike had grown over the course of our brief marriage to the point where it made me uncomfortable to be in the same room with them. Mike, to his credit, was always polite, but he wasn't submissive like Marco, and that grated on Pazzo.

Anyway, Pazzo decided to throw me a birthday party in the wine room at the local bistro. It's a private dining room where the bottles are kept. Small and intimate, only seating 25 or so, but clearly visible to the main dining room. Like eating in a fishbowl. I cringed inside about being on display and being the center of attention on my birthday. I hate to make a fuss about my birthday. And 52 didn't seem like a birthday of any significance.

Of course, I forgot for a moment that my birthday wasn't really about me, it was about Pazzo posing as the perfect husband, devoted and doting on his beloved wife on her birthday. And what better venue than a *private* dining room in plain view of a roomful of well-heeled diners? Like dinner theater, starring Pazzo. The lighting is perfect and the audience is pre-qualified, due to the high-end nature of the restaurant. Close your eyes and just imagine the scene for a moment.

As happy pockets of people tucked into their braised short rib gnocchi, followed by crispy skin duck breast with pomegranate molasses and a side of the bistro's famous glazed Brussels sprouts, they could glance over at Pazzo basking in the warm glow of his adoring wife, surrounded by a golden ring of glittering friends and marvel about our charmed marriage.

My husband gathered phone numbers from me for all of my friends and personally called them rather than sending invitations in the mail or even via email. He wanted the spotlight as party planner. And now he had my friends' numbers in his phone, which he didn't hesitate to use later after I left him.

Pazzo called and chatted everyone up. I have this one friend who has health problems and couldn't commit, not knowing how she would feel on the actual date of the dinner party. My husband was not having any of that. He gave her a deadline of several days later and called her back, badgering her for an answer, because he needed a headcount and didn't want to hold her place when he could invite someone else on my list.

This was to be an exclusive gathering with him as the maestro, conducting the party like a concert. He selected the menu, chose the wines, and ordered flowers. I had actually contracted giardia at Universal Studios, which is pretty much a third-world country, and would be unable to drink on my own birthday due to the antibiotics. In fact, I hadn't felt well since our return and was not feeling the least bit celebratory.

But I rallied the night of the party. My sister and her

husband drove over from Memphis, my childhood bestie and her husband came up from Birmingham. It was a convivial gathering of old friends with me at the center of it. And Pazzo, of course. My son was not able to be there for some reason. And not being able to anesthetize myself with alcohol, I found the evening especially tedious as Pazzo held forth, giggling giddily and watching me watch him, gauging my reactions to his performance.

Let me just say I'm not a complete ingrate. I was deeply touched by the turnout of my friends for this seemingly insignificant un-birthday of sorts. I felt like it was an imposition somehow. That's how low my self-esteem was. And I didn't feel good. And I wondered again to myself, *if I'm as awful as my husband says I am, how am I blessed with such amazing friends?* It was a dichotomy I couldn't quite reconcile in my brain.

I dutifully gave a toast to all my friends, especially my sister, and most of all my darling husband for orchestrating such a wonderful celebration.

My birthday extravaganza was followed by Pazzo's benefit concert for the launch of his new album, entitled *Black Soul*, which was also the name of the title song.

Roxie had recently taken up belly dancing, and she brought those seductive movements to the stage now. She wore snake bracelets encircling her creamy soft upper arms and wrapped a belled scarf around her soft midriff. She took to playing those little finger cymbals—*zills* they're called in Turkish, and *sajat* in Arabic. Tiny Tibetan *tingsha* bells.

As she sang "Black Soul," Roxie would click her clamshell bells together and sway her ample hips and warble her voice. It was mesmerizing. And the song was unlike anything Pazzo had ever written and arranged. He called it an earworm meaning you couldn't get it out of your head. I added the single to my yoga playlist and was proud of my husband's creativity.

"I can see your Black Soul
Deep within your shattered heart
Let me kiss your broken parts
My love will make you whole"

At the time I thought it was a love song of sorts. I don't remember all the lyrics but the gist was that Pazzo, as the songwriter, could love someone back together again. I wonder now if the black soul was his own instead of a lover's. And the song was projection. He wanted to be loved and made whole, despite his dark heart, which he kept in the shadows, obscured and hidden. Except when he didn't.

He asked if I would leverage my mad PR skills to promote his album. Here was the implicit quid pro quo that defined our relationship. *I threw you a party, so now you will plan my album launch.*

I sprang into action. We scheduled a Valentine's Day concert at a local performance venue, not too big, not too small. My goal was to fill it. I enlisted a graphic designer friend of mine to create a flyer and social skins for Pride of Lions's Facebook and Instagram accounts. We decided to donate proceeds from the cover charge to The Love Pantry, a local charity that feeds the homeless. The venue agreed to donate their portion of the proceeds as well. There was a nice love gift tie in for Valentine's Day. I pitched the music writer who covered big name acts and Big Ears Festival, the arty, upscale companion to Bonnaroo.

Pride of Lions got a nice feature story leading up to the concert. I placed the benefit on all the local entertainment event calendars and created a Facebook Event for it. Did a few boosted posts to a highly targeted hyperlocal demographic. I invited all my friends to stop by, before or after their own Valentine celebrations. Maybe Marco was with Ivy that night? Or maybe we got a sitter. I simply don't recall. But I donned a sexy top I'd purchased in Cyprus on a trip with Monika, who owned a home there with her Greek-Cypriot husband. I paired my exotic beaded bustier with low-slung, boot-cut jeans and my favorite fringed cowboy boots and worked the crowd like a boss.

My girlfriends and I danced in front of the band and sang along with the songs as best we could—I never could catch all of Pazzo's overwrought lyrics. But we sang and danced ourselves into a frenzy and then the opening strains of "Black Soul" began. He had a full band backing Roxie, had imported some serious guitarists from Nashville and even a Ravi Shankar-style sitar player to provide an authentic Eastern flavor.

The venue was packed. Pazzo was playing his sparkly red Strat, named after me, and beaming at me benevolently from the stage as he made love to his guitar. The heavy-lifting riffs were coming from an old, weathered Nashville artist who often joined Pride of Lions to jam when he wasn't fronting his own band. He, too, was gazing at me and later told Pazzo he loved it when I came to concerts.

I was the ideal groupie in every sense of the word—Pazzo had admonished me *never* to use that word, as everyone in the business knew that meant you were sleeping with the musicians. I thought it just meant being a fan. But in this case, it was true either way, as I was Pazzo's groupie, his band's loyal follower and promoter, having had input on song lyrics and artwork for the album cover. He had wanted to dedicate this first album to me, but I demurred, saying that wasn't fair to his fellow band members, who had been with him longer than I had.

I trance danced, sweating profusely, perspiration running down my cleavage and between my shoulder blades. My hair was wet. I had my concert flask tucked in my boot, filled with single-malt Scotch, sneaking sips and feeling the alcohol burn down my throat to the tips of my fingers and toes. I felt warm and content in that moment. Twirling around like a little girl. Who had ever done that for me? Spun me around in a circle, holding me by my hands? Maybe my father? Or had I only longed for it. Imagined it. Seen it in slow-mo on TV commercials.

I felt dizzy and delirious with happiness. That's what love feels like, yes?

It was dangerous and sexy and foreboding. Thrilling even. Who would let go of whose hands first? Who would go spinning out of control?

Winter melted into Spring. Mike finished his freshman year at college and prepared to move into an apartment with a friend for his sophomore year. Pazzo was keen to capitalize on this life event to grab Mike's room for Marco, whom Pazzo claimed had always coveted it.

I broached the subject to Mike, who said he didn't care since he was moving out anyway. But it hurt this mother's heart. I felt that my husband was trying to erase Mike from our family and replace him with Marco. Taking his room had huge significance for me. But I went along to avoid a blowup.

Picking Marco up after school one afternoon, I told him the good news.

"You get to have Mike's room now that he's moving out. Aren't you excited?"

Marco's face fell. He looked to be on the verge of tears, an expression I'd come to easily recognize.

"But I *love* my room," he stammered, trying to hold back big sobs. "Do I have to move?"

This child of change liked the stability of his room, the comfort of his routines. With everything that had happened in his life over the last year or so, moving schools, moving houses, getting a new stepmother and stepbrother, he wanted as little change as possible. Children hate change. Why didn't this neuropsychologist father know that?

"Of course, you don't have to move, sweetie. I thought you wanted to. That's what your dad said," I explained, trying to calm him down so we could get to swim lessons without a meltdown.

"I never said that. *He* wanted me to have Mike's room, not me," Marco blubbered bitterly, giving into the sorrow of being misunderstood and misrepresented by his own father. Again.

Turns out Pazzo had lied to me about Marco's wishes in order to claim the room he had always wanted for *his* child, and to gently efface *my* child from our lives. I died a little inside, just thinking about this. And when I confronted him later, he smoothly explained it away, saying Marco must have changed his mind. No big deal. I watched my son move out, with tears in my eyes, his empty room staying empty until my husband decided it would be a great place to store his guitar collection, as if the guitar closet and the upstairs office weren't enough. He was like a dog peeing on the bushes where another dog had been, staking his claim, marking—and expanding—his territory.

Something Pazzo liked to do and didn't mind spending money on was going to concerts. He'd always couch it as a surprise for me, but it was his personal indulgence. I was his sidekick. He'd even wear shades and some sort of cool jacket to the venue, like the one he bought at Lansky's in Memphis. People would stop us and ask if he was with the band. He *loved* that. Would just smile and shake his head while casually mentioning that he was a musician and a producer. I guess that made me his groupie.

We went to see the Rolling Stones in Chicago, Justin Timberlake in Nashville, and Madonna in D.C. These were good times. Pazzo was at his best away from Marco and work. These weekend getaways reminded me of our dating days and the fun we'd had, just the two of us. He'd get tickets up close to the stage with special VIP passes. We'd stay in cool hotels and eat at upscale restaurants. He'd drop thousands of dollars on these weekends without a second thought.

Then he'd come home and happily write songs and track down special, vintage, or otherwise rare guitars online. He'd buy them on eBay or from dealers. Fenders, Gibsons, Gretsches, and whatever else is sacred to guitar lovers. He'd tell me their provenance and lovingly show me all the features that made them special. The one he'd named after me was a bright candy-apple red Stratocaster with sparkles in the paint. And I loved him again in those moments, lost in his music. It made him tender and passionate, and we'd christen these guitars in intimate moments.

Again, there were pictures, always pictures of things I'd rather keep private. And lewd acts he'd ask me to perform with these instruments so he could take these vivid memories with him on stage where he was happiest, sweating and strumming and jumping like an overaged punk rocker. Other than sex, music was his only other creative outlet, his religion, and his release.

That summer was my 35th high school reunion. I'm not crazy about reunions. I think only people who move away get all fired up about coming back to town and reliving their high school days. While I loved that time of my life, I don't feel the need to relive it. I'd skipped my last reunion, being momentarily single—I think Peter and I were taking a break—and having braces at the time. It was a notable low point of my life. And one of my high school buddies had given me shit about not going.

"A lot of people worked really hard on this reunion, Jennifer," she'd nagged. "The least you can do is show up."

Wow, that *really* made me want to attend. Not.

Actually, I was sort of looking forward to introducing my new husband to the old gang. But, somewhere in the back of my mind, I worried that I'd be self-conscious with Pazzo there, unable to be myself and be in the moment, aware of his constantly watching me and judging my behavior.

I pulled out a red raw-silk dress I'd had for years and had actually worn to our 20th reunion or maybe the 25th. I'd bought it in the dress shop at The Greenbriar, and it was a memento of happier times from my first marriage, before the wheels came off the bus. It still fit, was expensive and timeless, and I felt pretty in it.

"You're not wearing *that*," Pazzo announced, upon seeing me in the dress.

"What? Why not? Don't you like it?"

"I can see your *nipples* through it," he said with disgust. "You're not leaving the house in that dress."

I didn't have a strapless bra. The dress was lined and textured. I thought you had to stare pretty hard at my breasts to make out the contour of my nipples, but he was adamant.

"Do you want me to wear a burka?" I asked, outraged that he thought he could tell me what to wear at my age. He'd often complained about my yoga clothes on Saturday mornings for the same reason. And white T-shirts. Anything that showed my breasts. Funny, it didn't seem to bother him at all when we were dating, and I wore halter tops with jeans and backless sundresses with nothing underneath. But now that we were married, he felt entitled to dictate my wardrobe choices and preferred that I not show the cleavage he so enjoyed when we were alone together.

A heated argument ensued, with me finally agreeing to put Band-Aids over my bosoms under my dress so that we could go to the reunion, where he proceeded to button-hole one of my classmates and bend his ear on some financial scheme for the entire time. Except when he was stalking another friend of mine, who happened to have graduated from Michigan, one of Pazzo's alma maters. He felt the need to catch her and charm her and hold her in his web.

Mary Ellen wasn't having it.

"Excuse me, could you leave me alone please? I never get to see these people, and I'm here to spend time with them," she told him in no uncertain terms when he interrupted her conversation for the second or third time.

She'd been polite at first. And she still was. Just firm. I marveled at her well-defined personal boundaries and wished I could be more like her. And I was embarrassed that my husband was making a fool out of himself.

I danced and drank and had fun without him. For once he didn't shame me when we came home or tell me that I'd said the wrong thing or unwittingly offended someone with my oafish behavior. He didn't dare. These were *my* friends from childhood. I had no doubt of my place here. He knew he couldn't touch that.

The dry-cleaners ended up ruining that dress. It had pretty gold shell straps, and they squished one. I'd loved that dress for decades, but I threw it away now. It was ruined, and not just because of the strap.

It was about this time that I had the opportunity to go on another adventure. With my favorite client. This time it was an Alaskan cruise, and it wouldn't cost anything because we had bartered my services in exchange for the trip. My third time with this fun-loving, globe-trotting gang of kindly souls. I enjoyed their company. We were more friends now than work associates; the president and his wife having attended Pazzo's birthday party for me back in January. I'd never been to Alaska before, never been to the Pacific Northwest. We'd embark from Seattle, so I was excited to see that city as well. I started booking excursions for dog-sledding and glacier-viewing at our ports of call.

"But we can't go," said Pazzo. "Marco can't miss school."

"Sweetie, it's an adult trip," I answered, shuddering inwardly at the thought of Marco's special needs taking center stage for the entire cruise. Pazzo always wanted to include Marco where he didn't belong and didn't want to be.

"Well, I can't miss work."

"I understand. I was thinking you'd stay home with Marco and I'd go by myself."

Silence. More silence. And then the storm clouds gathered on Pazzo's brow and burst into a shower of abuse. Picture those animated faces of clouds on the Internet, cumulonimbus cheeks puffed out, blowing hot air. Or perhaps the Wizard of Oz, screaming at Dorothy. Fantastically green, bloated, angry. *I am Oz, the great and terrible.*

"How *dare* you go on this trip without me? I thought we were a family? You know I've *always* wanted to go to Alaska."

This was the first I'd heard of that. He'd never mentioned wanting to go to Alaska before. Besides, we both knew he hated to fly and hated to leave work. Really, if we're being honest, other than weekends away to catch concerts, he hated to travel.

"Well, we can go back as a family some time. This way, I can check it out and see all the fun things to do and we can go back together," I suggested hopefully.

Surely he was not going to rain on my parade again. Not squash this opportunity. Something in me snapped. I wasn't going to let him have his way on this. It was a line in the sand for me. I'd briefly awakened from my Pazzo-induced stupor to remember he was my husband, not my captor, and he couldn't keep me from going if I wanted to go. And I wanted to go.

I dropped the subject and continued to make plans for the trip. We simply didn't discuss it. The air was thick with tension. You could cut it with a butter knife. Nothing pleased him.

Dinner was either too cold for Pazzo or too hot for Marco.

Salmon, again and again, because Pazzo wanted to eat *heart-healthy*. Although I'd no sooner cleared the table than he was in the pantry, riffling through sleeves of Chips Ahoy and Oreos, not even bothering to put the cookies on a plate or turn on the light. He just stood in there and grazed like a pig at the trough.

He'd always been ravenous, insatiable really, when it came to food. I'd make a meatloaf and think we'd eat on it for a week. Pazzo would inhale it in one sitting. He was a sperm whale on a deep dive, vacuuming up thousands of pounds of krill, along with the occasional old boot and spare tire. Pazzo consumed, subsumed, enveloped everything in his path.

His relationship with food was proprietary, primal even. He'd eat food off my plate, in some sort of show of dominance, as if to say, *What's yours is mine.* And it wasn't just food that was his. He took up physical space. Spread his stuff into every closet and cubby like a noxious fog. Our cabinets were full of Pazzo's CD collections. Our garage was full of tools he never used and bikes he never rode, along with band equipment—speakers, woofers, and tweeters. You already know about his guitar collection housed now in the upstairs office and Mike's old bedroom, as well as the designated guitar closet. Pazzo spread like lava through the house.

He habitually put things in my purse, his car keys, his wallet. Simultaneously lightening his own load and weighing me down with extensions of himself. I was his Sherpa, his pack mule, his whore, and his handmaid.

Pazzo's weight ballooned. He didn't sleep, preferring to watch obscure videos of old-school soul singers and British pop stars. He stayed up all night working or writing songs, or as I found out after our divorce, trolling Match.com and

Facebook for fresh meat. A divorced friend of mine later asked me if this was my husband, someone who had messaged her, "You have a beautiful face, but I wonder what your laugh sounds like?"

He ate his anger away. Complained about his health, his heart in particular. Still listed to the left as he shoveled in his dinner. Yelled at Marco the whole time for the slightest things. Marco didn't finish his milk. Marco dropped his fork. Marco played with his food. I sipped my dinner of chardonnay and bided my time. I needed a break from Pazzo. This trip would my chance to get away from the drudgery and hatefulness that had become my life. Cinderella needed some me time.

He complained about money, but since the trip was free he couldn't say much about that. Just that he was cutting my weekly household allowance, and that all his friends couldn't believe how much of his money I spent and that I wouldn't contribute to household expenses and how selfish that was. He'd often do this—invoke some Greek chorus of others—to validate his opinions of my behavior.

"I'm paying for Mike's college with my savings and paying for all his other expenses with the income from my consulting work," I patiently explained for the umpteenth time. I'd even taken to paying for my hair appointments and incidentals, clothes, anything that wasn't for Marco and Pazzo, who could eat through $200 a week of groceries and sweat through $200 a week of dry-cleaning.

And I thought, *At this rate I'm going to run out of money, and then I really will be trapped in this marriage.* The thought frightened me, both because I'd been in this situation before and because I'd actually thought it.

"Shrink can't believe you would even think of going to Alaska without Marco and me. Says you're really selfish," my husband opined. "Shrink" was the genderless name he'd given his therapist, whom he'd recently started seeing again. Or so he said. Hell, maybe he was "Shrink" and there was no therapist. I was beginning to doubt everything he said.

Red flag.

Narcissists use a form of psychological intimidation, called "gas-lighting," where they present false information to their victims, which makes them doubt their own memory, perception, and even sanity.

In the end, I did go to Alaska. And it was the beginning of the end. The end of my ill-fated marriage to Pazzo that had been a long time coming. But my husband wasn't going to let me go without a fight.

Once we were at sea, there were days without Wi-Fi. Blissful days when I didn't have to think about my husband's irrational anger or respond to his snide texts. Then when we got to our ports of call, the texts would tumble in—*ping, ping, ping*—a slot machine of hateful messages. I'd listen to his voicemails, and their escalating tone of exasperation. He was no longer masking his monster side. Dr. Jekyll was full-on Mr. Hyde. I could feel the cool breeze through the phone line.

"Call me *Now!*" he'd snarl into the phone. Then *click*. He'd hang up.

It was our one-year anniversary, and I was in Juneau, where the ship had docked for the day. I was dining on the *Best. Salmon. Ever.* at the Twisted Fish Company Alaskan Grill. Sipping wine in a window seat. By myself. Reflecting on the past year with Pazzo. The good, the bad, the ugly.

I didn't want to return his calls, but I sent out a hopeful little text into the ethersphere.

Happy Anniversary, sweet guy! I love you. XXOOO

I watched as the bubbles immediately began to dance on my screen, indicating he had received my message and was crafting one of his own in reply. I relaxed a little, allowed myself to breathe, let my shoulders unscrunch as I gazed out at the happy tourists and took another sip of my chardonnay.

This trip had been good for us, for Pazzo and me, I told myself. Good for our marriage. And my sanity. Paddling a canoe through Arctic waters to a blue ice cave, helicoptering to a remote outpost in the middle of a glacier, and riding behind a team of actual sled dogs, wandering around touristy port towns blissfully lost among the throngs in this gorgeous part of the planet. I felt refreshed and renewed somehow. Travel always has that effect on me.

Ping. Ping. I glanced down and scrolled to find his truncated messages.

"Jennifer, you'll have to do a much better job of showing that."

This was his answer to *I love you?*

"I love you too, but not in the same way that I used to."

My heart sank and my stomach clenched.

And, for the first time in our relationship I allowed myself to acknowledge what I was feeling. Fear. Real fear that I didn't know what he might do. That I had pushed him too far and lost him somehow. Something in him had snapped. And there was no going back.

Well, something in me snapped, too. It was as though scales fell from my eyes, and I saw Pazzo clearly for the very first time. And he knew it, too. This is why he didn't want me to go away without him. He *knew* I would get some clarity with distance. Without the constant mindscrew.

And in that instant of clarity, I knew what I had to do.

When I landed in Cherokee Hills it was late. I was bone tired and jet-lagged as I dragged my suitcase full of dirty laundry behind me across the airport parking lot to my car. Wrapped carefully in the sweaters and socks was an authentic Alaskan totem pole for Marco and an artist-signed polar bear sculpture for Pazzo. It was handmade of granite or some lovely white quartz on a marble base and weighed like a ton of bricks. I pictured it on his desk at work, providing gravitas to his office.

My husband had once told me of a polar bear statue he had visited regularly back in Michigan, consulting it like a silent god when he needed guidance. Touchstone. Spirit animal. Call it what you like. As an avowed atheist, it was the closest Pazzo came to prayer. My gift seemed to me like a fitting reminder of his halcyon school days, his myriad degrees, and how far he had come in his career.

I slipped into a dark house. No one had waited up for me, which was curious since Pazzo was such a night owl. I thought he'd be upstairs in the home office, headphones on, writing songs and picking urgently at his guitar. But no. So, I tiptoed in the dark into our bedroom, slipped out of my clothes and crawled into bed beside him. Before I could snuggle up to his polar bear shape, his voice cut through the darkness like a knife.

"I almost threw all your belongings out on the lawn."

Silence. I was speechless. Furious and mute. What was he talking about?

"And Mike's things? What were you going to do with them?" I stammered, feeling instantly protective of my son. Blinking back angry tears, I reminded myself that I owned this house, not Pazzo. And yet, he had clearly given this a lot of thought.

"I talked to Shrink, and I'm reducing your weekly household allowance. No one can believe how much money you spend. And by the way, everyone agrees how selfish it was of you to leave me to go on this trip. Cruel even. You never think of anyone but yourself."

Shrink. No one. Everyone.

I turned away from him and curled myself into a ball. I was shivering not from cold but from fury. And I resolved in that moment to act on the thoughts I'd had in Alaska. I would leave Pazzo. I would run away before he could stop me. I would not be owned and treated like chattel. I would not be dehumanized and eradicated from my own life. I had given him my heart but he wanted my soul. He wanted to consume me, obliterate me, and punish me for the unpardonable sin of seeing him as he really was.

So long honey, baby. Where I'm bound, I can't tell. Goodbye's too good a word, babe.

The next morning I made Marco pancakes—his favorite—and gave him his totem pole. He wanted to take it to school, but his father wouldn't let him. Instead he found a special place for it among the detritus of his room, next to his beloved Lego Death Star. Pazzo seemed pleased with his polar bear, putting it on his dresser in our bedroom.

And so, our uneasy truce began.

There was freedom in knowing I had a plan now. I began to play a role in order to put my plan into action. Whatever he wanted, whatever he said, I was all, *Yes dear that sounds lovely.* You'd think my sudden surrender and acquiescence would have made him suspicious, but instead it fed his ego. He felt vindicated in his righteous anger at my having left him for Alaska. He thought I had turned over a new leaf and was committed to showing him the proper deference and respect, catering to his every whim and being subservient to him in all things. Trying to "do a better job" of showing my love for him.

Dinner was on the table every night at six, just as he liked it, leaning hard to the left as he ate his salad. I filled the pantry with Chips Ahoy and Oreos for his nightly post-salmon-and-broccoli binges. And I drank glass after glass of wine. One at dinner. One on the porch after I did the dishes and cleaned up while Pazzo and Marco struggled through Marco's homework together.

"I'm going for a walk; do you want to come?" I'd ask them both as I took Hank out for a lap around the neighborhood. They rarely joined us, which was fine with me.

I was extra sweet to Marco, already feeling guilty about leaving him alone with Pazzo. I was a buffer between them, bridging the uneasy gap between Pazzo's unrealistic expectations and anger and Marco's brokenness and inadequacies. He just wanted to be loved for who he was, like all of us. But Pazzo couldn't love Marco. He wasn't perfect enough. We had that in common, Marco and me.

Swimming lessons continued. Pazzo still went to Nashville to work and gig. He was going back and forth to Detroit now, with Roxie, to record his next album. Marco woke up one night during a storm and came to my room glowing from fear. He was white as Elmer's glue, an even more translucent shade of pale than usual. He was rocking his upper body back and forth and flailing his arms like a little robot boy. I couldn't calm him. This was his coping mechanism for night terrors and anxiety.

"I want my dad. I want my dad," Marco cried over and over again.

So, we called him, both of us hoping Pazzo would calm him down and make it all better.

Pazzo was gruff on the phone, angry at Marco for being such a mess. I couldn't hear what he was saying to Marco, but I heard the stern tone of his voice and saw Marco's tears.

We went back to Marco's room and I read aloud to him for a while, but he never closed his eyes.

I usually enjoyed sleeping in Pazzo's big king-sized bed when he was away, knowing I wouldn't be bothered for sex, but that night I lay awake worrying about Marco, who slept through his alarm the next morning. He was a zombie at breakfast, falling asleep in his pancakes, raccoon rings under his eyes. I dropped him off at school, knowing he would have a terrible day.

Then I went to the condo I'd rented on the down-low and took a couple of plates, some flatware, some clothes. And I imagined a life without the burden of this pathetic little creature to care for. And I hated myself for feeling that way. But hadn't I raised my own son? Marco wasn't mine to raise. And I couldn't stay married to a monster just to care for the monster's son. It was like some awful fairy tale or parable. A woman is destined to a life of servitude and heaped with abuse, charged with caring for an unlovable child and his angry father in addition to her own beloved child, whom her husband resents, while also caring for her elderly parents. Was this my karma from a previous lifetime? A lesson I needed to learn? What was the moral of this story?

And shouldn't I be grateful to have a roof over my head and my health? Happiness is a choice, right? It's not contingent on your circumstances. So why did I feel this manic desire to flee from a life that others would be grateful to have?

Because my gut told me this was *not* my destiny. I *didn't* deserve it, and I wasn't going to take it. And I couldn't take Marco with me even if I wanted to. He wasn't mine to save.

I was in fight-or-flight mode. I had tried fighting with Pazzo but couldn't hold my own, much less *win* those fights. Why did every conversation have to be won or lost? Damn, it was exhausting. He beat me down with his barrage of caustic words and his superior argumentative techniques. He *loved* to argue. I hated it and had taken to falling at his feet, prostrate in absolute abject defeat. I'd lie down on the floor in front of him just to get him to stop yelling at me. Sometimes I'd sit back on my heels and bow to him, which he loathed. I'm not sure whether he was disgusted or infuriated. Not sure whether I was being sarcastic or authentic in my show of submission. It was at those moments that he'd ball up his fists in silent fury and walk away. I wondered when he would hit me—*When*, not *If*. Because it was only a matter of time before his abuse became physical. He was a violent man on the inside.

Did I really think he would hit me? No. He was too controlled for that. It would be too uncouth, too lowbrow, too obvious. He never even spanked Marco. His uber-liberal sensibilities didn't allow him to approve of corporal punishment. His abuse was more insidious, breaking me down from the inside out. Maybe Ivy wasn't always the mess she became. Maybe she was weak, and he just wore her down over the years with his Chinese water torture of verbal violence, and she turned to her own means of self-anesthetizing to escape him. Booze. Pills. Anything to numb the pain of his relentless onslaught. He destroyed Ivy and then blamed it on her so he could get custody of Marco. Maybe he even sought her out as a victim, smelling emotional blood in the shallows like a bull shark.

The couple Pazzo had dinner with the night after our first date, he told me later, said I was a crazy bitch and that he shouldn't date me. That hurt. I knew them casually and actually liked them. Wow.

It hurt that they said it, but it hurt even more that he would repeat it to me. Why would he tell me that, this man who loved me? What purpose did it serve? It seemed cruel. But that was his style, his way of validating his criticism. He claimed an ex-girlfriend told him the same thing about me.

Which begs the rational question of why didn't he listen? If I was so awful and he was warned, why did he marry me anyway? Something didn't add up. I knew it in my gut.

Why marry someone and then make her doubt her sanity, her worth, her value?

Because he wanted me to feel crazy and invalidate myself, so he could control me under the guise of caring husband. Just. Like. His. Father. It was the ultimate power trip for a controlling sadistic narcissist. And it meant I would never leave him. Like his brother Alfie had left him. Without warning. Without a word. Never to speak to him again. Inflicting the unforgivable narcissistic wound.

His mother was an invalid. His sister was becoming an invalid. Ivy was emotionally unstable.

And Ivy didn't leave him—he threw her out and kept her child.

Did I think he would hit me? Nah, but he might kill me.

If he couldn't beat me down into emotional submission with his barrage of poison words, he might actually poison me and make it look like an overdose of some kind or put a pillow over my face and say I died in my sleep. Anything to position himself as the long-suffering, devoted, attentive husband. After two divorces, perhaps widower might become him more in attracting his next victim. It might play well on the dating sites, making him an even more sympathetic character in his self-narrative.

I knew he would never let me leave. His ego couldn't withstand another abandonment. Like his brother Alfie's. Rejection was not an option. Pazzo wouldn't allow it. He couldn't abide being alone. Without love and sex and constant adoration. A beautiful wife to reflect on him and validate him as a human being instead of a soulless monster. And he needed someone to raise his child for him.

These were the thoughts running through my mind. Hell, maybe I was crazy.

But lately, since Alaska, I'd let his words roll off me like I was made of satin instead of Velcro. I was slowly regaining my power and biding my time.

The night before I ran away I came home from teaching yoga, determined to spend one last evening with my husband. I wanted to see if there was anything left of the intermittent magic we had once shared. I imagined making love with him once last time and falling asleep in his arms. I wanted a gentle memory of him to take with me when I left.

I entered through the garage and saw the light on in the

upstairs office. I tiptoed up the steps, so as not to wake up Marco. Pazzo was at his desk, multiple screens open in front of him, headset on, guitar on his lap, composing, arranging, letting the music dance in his head, where he alone was songwriter, conductor, arranger, and lead guitarist. A one-man band.

He looked up and nodded abruptly, then went back to his work. I walked numbly back down the stairs. If I'd been looking for a reason to stay, I hadn't found it. I took off my yoga clothes, put on my pajamas and poured myself a glass of wine. Letting Hank out, I curled up in the wicker chair on the back porch and listened to the windchimes clatter in the cool autumn breeze.

In that moment, I knew there was no turning back.

Escape
&
Divorce

On Thursday morning, November 8, I made my escape. I fixed breakfast for Pazzo and Marco, packed Pazzo's lunch and Marco's as well as his midmorning snack—he was prone to sinking spells and his indulgent teachers had given special dispensation for him to nosh before lunch. I fed the cat and the dog. Made the beds. Did the dishes. Tidied up. Kissed Marco on the head and Pazzo on the mouth and told them I loved them. And I did. But I was also leaving.

The moving van was scheduled for 9 a.m., and I was hoping Pazzo didn't show up for his own post-breakfast indulgence. I was catlike in my nervousness.

I put letters on the counter for both of them, in individually addressed envelopes. I especially wanted Marco to know it wasn't his fault, and at the same time, I blamed him in Pazzo's letter, lest I unleash the Kraken of wrath by pointing the finger squarely at Pazzo. I was ashamed of my dissembling half-truths, my apparent inability to speak my truth, even in that moment of truth. I was trying to spare Pazzo's feelings even as I was leaving him, afraid to set him off, scared of what he might do.

〜

Dear Marco,

You are a bright, beautiful boy, and it has been a joy to be in your life these past few years. I've watched you grow and mature from a child into a young man. I wish I could stay around for the rest of your journey to adulthood, but I can't.

Remember when I told you life isn't fair? Well, it's true. Sometimes things happen that make no sense, and sometimes your heart breaks and you don't know how to fix it. That's how I feel right now. Please know that none of this is your fault. Some people just aren't cut out to be married. I guess I'm one of those people.

Now a word about your dad—He is the bravest, strongest, smartest man in the world and everything he does he does for you. So, take care of him for me, okay?

In the words of Winnie the Pooh, "Promise me you'll always remember: You're braver than you believe, and stronger than you seem, and smarter than you think."

Know that even though we are apart, you will always be with me in a special pocket of my heart.

I'm leaving Richard Parker with you and trusting him to your care. Hank will be with me, as he is not as self-sufficient as our orange tiger tabby ninja.

Be good. Brush your teeth. And keep reading.

I love you.

〜

Dearest Mike,

Thank you for loving me and for being my best friend.

You are brilliant and talented and funny and fun. You are my guitar hero, and I will always love you. But I can't raise your child. I've tried, and I just can't do it.

I don't like the person I've become in our marriage. I want to be happy again.

And I want to leave you with love. I cherish our relationship, the intimacy, the laughter, the little things and the larger-than-life way you give yourself completely to the people lucky enough to matter to you.

You have been supportive of my family, helping care for my parents and my son. You have made me feel beautiful and special and worthy. For all this and so much more, I am forever grateful.

Please let me go without anger, and do not try to contact me.

I wish you happiness and success and music, always music.

You are a wonderful father. Marco is so fortunate to have you. And I know, more than anyone, how hard parenting has been for you, due to extenuating circumstances. You don't deserve the heartache and misery. But life is not fair.

Know that I love you still and always will. Even though I couldn't say goodbye.

XXOOO

I took off my Tiffany wedding band and placed it carefully on top of Pazzo's envelope. I also left my Tiffany-blue mobile phone, having destroyed the sim chip. Six weeks in planning was about to come together in what I hoped was a perfectly executed exit strategy.

I took Hank to the condo I had rented and furnished. With a knot in my chest I left Richard Parker behind to rule the neighborhood and keep Marco company. I couldn't bear to coop him up in a condo nor could I keep him outside so near the road. There was a little raw lump in my throat at the thought of leaving behind my beloved companion of nearly a decade. Have I told you about my cat? Richard Parker had been with Mike and me for years before I married Pazzo. Marco had become particularly attached to him. Richard Parker was powerful and self-contained, serene and sure of himself. *He'll be fine,* I told myself through my tears.

Then, inexplicably, I cleaned up after the movers came. Swept away the dust bunnies where the sugar chest had been, vacuumed the carpet where it was pressed down from my grandmother's dresser. I left most of my belongings, not wanting to disrupt the household. I was scarred from the war zone Ivy had left in her wake when she left Pazzo; and I was determined not to do that to Marco. Figured we could sort all that out later.

We had a prenup after all, that said what was mine was mine and what was Pazzo's was Pazzo's. We were to keep the things we brought into the marriage. If either party wanted to buy out the other and stay in the house, that's what would happen. I assumed Pazzo would want to stay for Marco and that when and if he ever moved, I'd collect the rest of my things then. Naïve, I know—I mean I was walking out on him and I thought he'd be civil about personal belongings. I took my grandmother's portrait and Mike's. And not much else.

To this day I only have four place settings of silverware. Because I took half the set and left the other half for Pazzo and Marco, even though it was my flatware from before our marriage. I keep forgetting to get more. Occasionally I have friends over for dinner and have to wash the salad forks in order to serve dessert.

I'd arranged for Pazzo to be served with divorce papers that evening when he came home from work rather than at his office. I didn't want to embarrass him. I blocked him on all social accounts and via email. Opened a new email account that he didn't have. He didn't have my new phone number or know where I'd gone. I was safe and cozy in my little condo, my nest where I had landed.

I'd told Mike when he cleaned out his room for Marco that I was leaving and not to say anything and that I'd have the rest of his furniture delivered to the condo. He was incredulous, having no idea of Pazzo's angry, abusive side. He begged me just to talk to Pazzo, but I had given up on that strategy long ago, having talked myself blue in the face only to be shouted down and gaslighted. Mike was saddened for me, I could tell. But he was focused on school and leaving the nest anyway, so he did as I asked, for once.

A dear old childhood friend showed up to help me make my escape, and giddy after the stressful morning, we opened the bottle of Pouilly Fuisse I'd put in my empty condo fridge just for this purpose. I hadn't eaten and was already drunk on freedom, feeling secure with a tiny nest egg in the bank, even after paying the rent on the condo and buying new furniture. There were legal fees and moving expenses, but I allowed myself to be cautiously optimistic about the future. I had some clients. I could work now in peace and not be financially controlled by Pazzo.

I finally allowed myself to exhale. Felt like I'd been holding my breath for a year.

I was a bird let out of a cage. And I only now realized that the date of my departure was significant for another reason. November 8 was my grandmother's birthday. She was my guardian angel. She had been watching over me as I fled from an oppressive gloom into the crisp fall sunlight, the smell of damp leaves and the promise of a new life.

Things were quiet for a couple of weeks as I caught my breath in the in between. Mike was coming and going from campus and seemed to like his new room at the condo, complete with a private bathroom. He'd been a good sport sharing space with Marco. My neatnik only child, forced to contend with toddler-age-appropriate bath toys, not to mention a toothpaste-stained sink and feces-stained towels. Wiping his own bottom was something else Marco struggled with, and he sometimes used towels instead of toilet paper. Cringing as I type this.

I was soaking up my new-found freedom like a sea sponge, sleeping alone in a new bed on a new mattress, surrounded by clean surfaces and peaceful vibes. I especially enjoyed my tiny gated balcony, where I could leave Hank when I left, ensuring that he was entertained by passing traffic and that my new she-fortress was protected. I felt incognito, taking care to park behind a tree out front, imagining that Pazzo didn't know where I was and wouldn't find out.

Then the abusive letters started. Not from Pazzo but from his bulldog lawyer, who pointed out that I didn't hold Pazzo to the terms of our prenup because I didn't force him to pay me $50,000 when he sold his house, ergo, he was no longer bound by its terms. Of course he hadn't netted $50,000 after the sale and the money he did make went to pay his back taxes. But this loophole seemed to be enough to invalidate the entire agreement. I would not be getting any of my belongings back, not the family antiques or even the ordinary but no-less-special things I'd brought with me into our marriage.

There was a lovely Victorian English ceramic platter, creamy and crackled with tiny fissures from generations of use. It had some sort of woodland scene on it in a shade of cranberry. It had held our family's Thanksgiving turkeys for generations, my earliest memories of it at my grandmother's house and later on the sideboard in the dining room at my childhood home under the mural. It was kind of a toile-esque looking platter, substantial and imbued with festive memories. Why Pazzo would want it, I can't imagine. It was *my* family heirloom, probably of no real value to anyone outside my immediate family. And yet, his attorney made it clear that by *abandoning* my husband, I had forfeited my rights to everything in my house, even my own belongings.

There was the elegant 18th century burled walnut brandy board that Steve and I had bought at an antique show in Nashville before Mike was born. We were in his Porsche at the time and couldn't bring it home, so the dealers, based somewhere in Ohio, hand delivered it to our door several months later. I was charmed by the faux door that was really a deep drawer with a lock and key for housing expensive spirits back in colonial days. I polished it to a gleaming sheen and lovingly moved it from house to house in the early days of my first marriage. It was one of the few fine pieces we didn't sell off to pay off *his* back taxes. *Yes, this seems to be a recurring theme for me.*

I guess my beloved brandy board graces Pazzo's dining room now in his new life with his new wife.

The list goes on and on, but I couldn't bear to keep track. Oriental rugs that had belonged my parents. More treasures my first husband and I collected, antique furniture and silver from Charleston, artwork and collectibles from our travels abroad, including a Russian icon I smuggled back in my suitcase from St. Petersburg. All the treasures of my first marriage and my childhood, my mother's childhood and my grandmother's. I guess these things legitimized Pazzo in some way. Gave him a false patrician background, appropriated memories from someone else's life, like the lyrics of his songs. His shallow empty soul is a suction cup for other people's lives and stories, their heartaches and blessings. He cannot feel, but he can steal other people's stories, lives, and souls.

Or maybe they're just the spoils of war.

I'm still missing things, all these years later, my grandmother's grapefruit spoons, the little oil painting I bought in Asheville with Peter, my favorite wooden-handled melon baller. And yet, my belongings were tainted somehow. They'd become radioactive from exposure to Pazzo. Even my most precious personal possessions were damaged goods, just like my psyche. I would forever associate everything in that house with him and that era of awfulness.

I was the trapped fox that gnaws off its own foot to escape. Freedom at all costs. Even if you leave part of yourself behind.

The house was to be put on the market, according to Pazzo's lawyer. Pazzo and Marco wouldn't be staying. Furthermore, Pazzo would no longer pay the mortgage even while they were still living there. I could no longer access my own house, even to get my clothes, and I couldn't evict them either. But I was on the hook for the mortgage payments.

My carefully executed dream escape was turning into a nightmare. Pazzo's tentacles reached beyond the walls of the house we had shared and tethered me still. His slimy, sticky grasp extended beyond time and space. He had supernatural powers, and I feared I could never break free of his hold. Having his attorney verbally assault me in her emails to my attorney was a stroke of narcissistic genius. Pazzo knew how emotionally fragile I had become. How sentimental I was and how conflicted I felt for leaving. He knew his hurtful words stung like acid. And I could hear his evil voice in every line of every email. Feel his loathing in every carefully crafted toxic sentence.

These emails would bring me to my knees, reliving all the awful gaslighting of our marriage, seeing me described through Pazzo's discerning and terrifying lens.

My no-nonsense lawyer would answer Pazzo's attorney's vitriolic diatribes in one sentence.

"I have received your email and have communicated your terms to my client."

My lawyer was a no bullshit kinda gal. She reasoned, like a feminist therapist, that I should be glad I escaped with my life and that *stuff* didn't matter. She advised me to pick my battles.

Most bizarre of all, still trying to control me financially, Pazzo insisted that I pay him $60,000 to leave my house, regardless of what the sale price was. His lawyer estimated that would be half of the equity, and that he was entitled to it, despite the fact that he didn't own the house. And by not making the mortgage payments, he was crippling me financially, forcing me to make rent payments on my new condo in addition to paying the mortgage, which I could not afford. And I was not allowed back in the house to stage it for resale or work with the Realtor. And he could refuse showing at will if it didn't suit him. I was hemorrhaging what little savings I had left.

I was crying a lot, not eating or sleeping. Becoming hysterical and even suicidal. I reasoned that death would be my only escape from Pazzo and his endless emotional—and now—financial torment. He was going to take me down with him. Destroy me for leaving him. He ranted on Facebook and called my friends. Then, one night I came home to find my red stilettos with the champagne cork placed just so, right outside the locked wrought-iron gate that enclosed my balcony and my front door. Hank was sitting placidly beside the gate. Of course, my sweet dog wouldn't have barked at Pazzo. Had probably let him pat his silky chocolate head between the bars, licking his former master's hand in his guileless canine way.

It was a particularly personal message. No note necessary. I knew who had put my shoes there. Pazzo knew it wouldn't sound ominous or threatening in the retelling. *My estranged husband left a pair of my shoes by my door.* It wasn't exactly a horse's head in my bed. But the message was clear to me. It told me he knew *exactly* where I lived and I wasn't free at all, and he was evoking our former intimacy as the ultimate mindscrew, as if to say: *Do you remember when—because I do. And I still own you, body and soul. You will never be free from me.*

I remembered once making love with Pazzo back when we were still dating. He was on top of me, grunting and sweating, actually dripping droplets of perspiration on me. After his noisy and dramatic climax, he looked down and gently stroked my face, placing both of his palms on my cheeks. Then he slid his hands down to my throat and squeezed. Not too hard. Not terribly hard. Not enough to freak me out. But enough to startle me and make me question his expression of ecstasy and adoration, or was it something else? He could see through my eyes to the back of my brain, but when I looked in his eyes, I saw nothing. No expression whatsoever.

It only lasted a moment, the tightening of his soft, meaty hands around my neck. I gasped and then he smiled and laughed and kissed my forehead playfully, before rolling off me and onto his back.

"I'm crazy about you, Jennifer. I don't know what I'd do if you ever left me."

He patted his furry chest and I snuggled under his arm and fell asleep with my face in his fur, breathing in his particular musk and feeling grateful for his love. Craving safety and security and wanting so to be taken care of, after a life spent fending for myself and caring for others. He was a big temperamental bear, irrational and unpredictable, but he was *my* bear. And he would protect me and defend me to the death from anyone who ever tried to hurt me.

My Sicilian savior. Fierce. Mercurial. Brilliant. Brave.

But who would protect me from Pazzo?

The house eventually sold, but I lost money after the upfront payout to Pazzo. It took a couple of months for the sale to close, during which time my lawyer negotiated that Pazzo pay half of the mortgage since he and Marco still resided at the house. When I complained at the unjustness of the arrangement, she shut me down hard.

"No judge in the world is going to evict a father and his minor son. There's nothing you can do about it. Decide what matters and move on."

Yes sir, I mean ma'am.

She was the ultimate in tough love, part attorney, part life coach, this daughter of a brigadier general, having served in the Army herself after a life as a military brat. She was hard as a hammer and cool as the frost that coated my windshield in the morning now, no more heated garage in a gated community. Just an open parking lot beneath my gated balcony.

I would sneak over to my old neighborhood a couple of times a week to fellowship with my beloved cat, whom I had left behind for Marco and because I couldn't bear to confine him to the condo. He'd be perched on the smooth stone walls outside our neighbor's house like the lions outside the New York Public Library or perhaps the Great Sphinx of Giza, simultaneously benevolent and ferocious. Richard Parker is the essence of chill. He'd sit at the highest point in the gated community. Calmly surveying his kingdom. Then he'd gracefully meander down the steps when he saw me pull around the circle in the cul de sac. My sweet neighbors had agreed to feed him and look after him in case Pazzo and Marco were neglectful.

But my cat was as stout and sleek as ever, the ultimate survivor, always with a back-up family and a plan, supremely independent and serene. I envied him that. I'd bring him treats and woozle his neck and sit on the steps across the street from Casa Pazzo, numb and crying and afraid. But with no regrets about leaving. He could take my money and my security, undermine my self-esteem and collapse my confidence, but he couldn't destroy me. Stuff was just stuff. And I could make more money, even if I needed to work at Starbucks for health insurance and to supplement my consulting income. I watched my cat calmly groom himself in the November sunlight and I felt it, too. My calm was my responsibility. My equanimity was within my own control. I knew this from yoga, of course, but I'd been on the verge lately, living raw and exposed like a live wire after a lightning strike.

I took a big gulp of that cold November air and held it in my lungs before exhaling. I gazed at the cerulean sky, closing my eyes and feeling the warmth of the impartial sunlight on my eyelids. It didn't take sides. Neither did the wind which blew crunchy leaves across the pavement and caused them to dance like paper dolls made of crumpled up grocery bags.

It was up to me to move on. It wasn't about winning. Clearly Pazzo had won. He'd already bought a new (to him) vintage Jaguar with the 60-grand settlement. It was both a balm to his wounded pride and a prop for his next pursuit. He loved the game of love. His hunger for conquest was insatiable. The subsequent relationship was inconsequential.

Instinctively, I scooped up my cat and took him back to the condo, where he greeted Hank coolly, like a bored teenager acknowledging a younger sibling. He sniffed about daintily and then sat down in a sun puddle and closed his eyes.

Letting Go & Moving On

It's been five years to the day since I walked out on Pazzo. And I'm still not sure what happened, how I was lured into his cult of one. He was like the cartoon snake in *The Jungle Book*. Big googly eyes that hypnotized me and put me to sleep for a couple of years. I still don't know how he did it. Dulled my senses and lulled me into an altered state of semi-consciousness. *Trust in me. Just in me. Shut your eyes. Trust in me.*

They say narcissists prey on weak people who worship them and have the same belief that only some people are *worthy*. I never considered myself weak, but I have been plagued by a lifetime of feeling unworthy and *not enough*. And, I think on some level, I was tired of being strong and brave and fixing and caring for and doing and giving. I wanted to be taken care of.

Pazzo remarried shortly after we divorced. A lovely young woman called Elise. I can only assume he met her on an online dating site. *Your face is beautiful, but I wonder what your laugh sounds like?*

A well-intentioned friend of mine mentioned that she'd seen my ex with a young woman at brunch one Saturday morning, holding hands across the table. She was pretty and young, with long brown hair.

"I guess he wasted no time getting back in the dating game," I remarked, surprised by how much her casual observation hurt me.

"Oh no, y'all were still married at the time. I remember," she said pointedly.

I was stung. And more than a little deflated. By the revelation and by her need to point that out to me. I think she was commiserating, a fellow divorcee, navigating the shark-filled waters of singledom *at a certain age.* But it hurt more than it should've. *She doesn't know when I left him. Why is she telling me this anyway?* When I thought more about it, I realized it was probably true. All those times he called to see where I was and when I was coming home. I thought he was checking up on me, which he was. Was he also covering his bases, building his alibis, timing his dalliances?

Narcissists will ultimately cheat on you, a psychologist friend had told me. They're wired differently. It's like they can't help it. They have to feed their need for constant adoration. For some it's the quest, for others it's the conquest. But they *need* it.

Maybe he started cheating on me when I went to Alaska. Maybe it was when I got back and checked out emotionally, going through the motions of our marriage, anesthetized by copious amounts of Pinot Grigio.

But if that's true, why did he still want me? Why the stilettos on my balcony? Or was it more about the *leaving* than wanting me to stay. Maybe it was the quest all over again.

Wooing and winning me back, only to destroy me. To finish what he had begun. Or to leave me instead. To rewrite the ending of our love story and salve his wounded id.

Friends of mine followed Pazzo's courtship of Elise on Facebook. Apparently he referred to her as "my lady" in posts, which I thought was really cheesy. Since I had blocked Pazzo I could no longer see his page, but I did see Elise's. She was a beautiful brunette with golden eyes—like the chatoyant gemstone, tiger's eye. Exactly 20 years younger than Pazzo and me, according to the "About" section that listed her high school graduation date. He took her to all our favorite haunts. It was as if he was recreating our relationship, retelling the story of us, but he had recast the lead, replaced me in our romance.

There was the Valentine's Day post of Pazzo and Elise at the mountain lodge where we spent our wedding night—ironically it had burned down and been rebuilt in between. Purified by fire, perhaps. There were pictures of them sailing at Mackinac Island. Finally, an outdoor wedding ceremony, just the two of them, by the water somewhere. She looked guileless and gorgeous in a cinched-waist dress with a black long-sleeved bodice. Her wedding gown had a plunging neckline and an elegantly pleated gold-lamé skirt. Non-traditional. Demure yet daring. I thought it was kinda badass, actually. She didn't look *bridal* in any sense of the word, but then this would be Pazzo's fourth wedding, so what difference did it make? The sunlight glinted off her skirt, and she was smiling in the pictures, backlit against the dazzling pointillist horizon where sea meets sky.

In one photo, Pazzo had scooped Elise up in his arms and was gazing adoringly down at her face, as her hair and her skirt swirled around them. He had, quite literally, swept her off her feet. She was his shiny new prize, his latest trophy wife. A more exotic, less conventional Colleen, and I secretly hoped she had the strength to withstand him. To marry him without losing herself.

Marrying my best friend, she had captioned the photo.

He was wearing the same suit he wore at our wedding.

I checked her Facebook page again from time to time. There were no posts with Marco, no mention of family, no updates after the wedding photos and sailing pictures. Just her bio picture, staring straight at the camera, her dark hair falling like curtains on either side of her pretty face.

Then I happened to check again over Christmas, and her photos had been carefully scrubbed of all Pazzo references. No pictures, no mentions. But she had posted a picture of three little gingerbread cookies and captioned it: *Pazzo Christmas family photo. Last night we had fun making gingerbread replicas of each other.*

There were three cookies all lined up on some sort of polished wood surface—*My brandy board?* I wondered. In front of a lovely tree, beside a mantle with three stockings. And above the mantle was an oil painting of mine, from before I married Pazzo, done for me by an artist friend, a childhood friend and later a flame. He had brought it to me at work, making a show of signing the back of the canvas for me.

It hung over my desk in my office until I left my job to become a fulltime mail-order bride for Pazzo. I had it elegantly framed at a local gallery. Pazzo, of course, tried to co-opt the friendship, inviting my free-spirited artist friend to join him at expensive dinners and subsequently buying a couple of pieces himself. Holden, my long-haired leather clad friend delivered the artwork on his motorcycle. He wasn't above taking Pazzo's money or drinking the $500 bottle of wine—Pazzo made sure to announce the price when the server arrived to show him the label. Then he did all that sniffing and swirling, which I found so pretentious and cringe-worthy. He was "cockblocking," as a guy friend of mine later described it. Showing Holden his superiority, demonstrating his façade of financial success and his supposed sophistication.

Holden smiled and gazed at me over the top of his glass as Pazzo made a toast. I think now that if he had taken my hand and led me out of the restaurant, I would have roared away with him on his bike into oblivion. Anywhere. Just away.

When I saw Elise's picture-perfect living room vignette, complete with a baby grand piano by the fireplace, gleaming hardwood floors, the soft neutral palette, with shades of ivory and grey on the wall, I couldn't take my eyes off the painting over the mantle.

Holden's painting for me. Hanging in the place of honor in the new Pazzo household. I'm quite sure Elise has no idea of its provenance. Knowing Pazzo, he lied about it or fabricated his own truth about the origins of the artwork. Someone had commented in the thread under Elise's Facebook post, "Send me a pic of your painting over the mantle. Love it!" Elise had "liked" the comment.

At first, I felt a wave of fury rush over me. I was livid. He's still the same parasite, sucking my soul, stealing my art, parsing my taste and style, and taking it as his own. Shapeshifting, soulless monster, pretending to be sensitive and artistic, hiding his base self. I thought again about all my treasured belongings I left behind when I was ordered not to return to my house. The things I had left so that Marco would feel safe. I hadn't wanted to rape and pillage the way Ivy had when she left Pazzo. So, I left my heart and soul in the house. And Pazzo took it with him when he went.

Still makes me mad. I feel violated. Used. Riled up. All over again.

And something else too. I feel erased. Invisible in my own life. Staring at a piece of myself hanging over the mantle in Pazzo's new house with his new wife and his new life.

When I dream of that time in my life, the Pazzo era, it's Marco's sad, pallid countenance that haunts me. His angular face, his eyes full of hurt. Cutting himself on his own broken edges. My guilt is like an extra five pounds I carry around. Making my clothes snug and my breath short, like a constant uncomfortableness. Something I just can't shed.

I relive the desperate little hug we shared the morning I left. When I knew I was going, but he didn't. My great escape. Leaving Jennifer. I ran away and never looked back. I couldn't take him with me because he wasn't mine to take, right? But my terrible guilt is mashed up with deep shame because I didn't *want* to take him. There, I've said it out loud.

Just the other night I awoke with a gasp from a night terror that felt so real because it could so easily happen. In my dream I was in the grocery store and saw Marco in the cereal aisle, as I had so many times before. But instead of the awkward overgrown carrot-topped grasshopper too old for the kiddie cart his mother blithely pushed as she sauntered along, Marco was a young man, of indeterminate teen years, standing upright, with the sullen, angry swagger of adolescents everywhere.

No more confetti-sprinkled toothpaste stains on his shirt. Pants zipped. Shoes still untied, but it could have been intentional, a look, rather than an oversight. His hair was dark like his father's but without the gray streaks. It was as though Marco had colored it, Gothlike, rather than his red hair having faded naturally to a muted auburn brown. Jet-black mussed mop, the color of Hank the Dog.

Marco had a defiant set to his jaw. Angry vibes radiating from him like a human sparkler. There was no trace of the lost little boy he had been. And yet, for some reason, I held out my arms and called his name, expecting him to run into them just as he had run into Pazzo's all those years ago when he burst from his mother's car in the driveway. Back when I first laid eyes on him.

But in my dream it didn't happen like that. When he caught sight of me, his eyes blazed with rage, and his face fell into a grimace. Balling his fists, he stormed toward me. His words hit me in the face like scalding water. *Why did you leave me behind?*

I once told Pazzo that I had a fantasy of just leaving my life and driving away—Thelma and Louise style, but not over a cliff—and starting over somewhere, in some small town. My dream was to live a quiet life. Full of books and yoga. Where nobody knows me and I can exist in peace.

I still have that dream.

Maybe I'll be a waitress or work at a Starbucks, although I'm getting a little long in the tooth and achy in the back for that now. Maybe I'll just keep writing and see where it takes me.

My son Mike, my beloved only child, is truly grown now into a fine young man who can take care of himself. My parents are gone from this world, recently reunited in paradise. And I want to see what else is out there for me besides taking care of other people.

Pazzo tried to spin my fantasy into being about him, leaving *him*. That was never it.

I left to escape *from* him. He was destroying me like a cancer, and I truly believed he would kill me, that his insidious verbal abuse and social isolation would turn into physical violence. He would beat me down just as he had Ivy and then paint me as a broken mess of my former self whom he tried to save from my untimely demise. I feared for my life. He'd make it look like suicide or an accidental death of some kind. He'd be the grieving widower and then start looking for his next Colleen to control. A search and destroy mission that will repeat itself as long as there are vulnerable women to prey on.

On my last birthday I received a package in the mail. The address label was typed but there were rabbit ears drawn along the edges, little bunny faces with penciled-in whiskers. Pazzo used to call me "Bunny." It was one of his early terms of endearment, along with "Goddess" and the blatantly objectifying and somewhat demeaning "Doll." *Bunny. Bunny. Bunny.*

He'd text me bunny faces in strings of what we referred to as "emoji salad," nonsensical messages comprised entirely of random emoji. I simultaneously smiled and shuddered at the memory.

Surely the package couldn't be from Pazzo. After all this time.

I struggled to get the lid off the cardboard tube, finally extracting the poster inside and unrolling it to find an image of a tiger, comprised entirely of words. It was text from *Life of Pi*, the fantasy adventure story by Yann Martel, that features an Indian boy named Pi and a Bengal tiger named Richard Parker, the namesake for my own beloved tiger tabby cat.

No note. Just the poster.

I've stopped trying to understand. Quit asking *why?* and *why me?* Have put it behind me as best I can. Some people are lucky at love, and some aren't. I've been blessed with friends and a beautiful son, if not with a singular soulmate. I've known love at times and lost it. Made bad choices, like Pazzo, and the men I've dated since him, all equally unavailable in their own way, either emotionally or physically, and all seeking to take advantage of me in some way.

There was the mysterious CIA agent I met on Bumble who was into D/s stuff and Cosplay and the married man who wanted to tie me to the bed. Let it be noted that I did not join in their deviant reindeer games. But I did date them and dance with their dark sides. And I could feel myself getting caught up in their webs of manipulation. Repeating old ingrained patterns, trying to please men who could never be pleased, trying to *earn* their love and loyalty in some misguided masochistic quest.

Red flag. Red flag.

"Secret Agent Man," as he was dubbed by my girlfriends and me for easy reference, always called me "Sugar" and was beguiled by my Southern-ness. I was a novelty for him in that regard.

He always texted in tidy bundles of words, with paragraph breaks in between to separate his thoughts. It struck me as odd at first, but now it makes perfect sense. Why should texts be run-on threads of emoji-punctuated babble—looking in the mirror here—when they can be organized into cogent blocks of incisive thoughts? God, he was smart. And achingly articulate. I'm a sucker for a beautiful mind, even when it's troubled or maybe especially then.

I think I overlooked his peculiar predilections—he once told me he fantasized about having two penises—for the sake of stimulating conversation.

I ran into Married Man at Starbucks over Christmas.

"I wasn't expecting to see you," I stammered distractedly, scanning the place for the guy I was supposed to be meeting, an old high school friend in town for the holidays.

"I bet you weren't," he replied, as we had recently had a text exchange in which I let him have it for being weak and hiding behind his wife's apron strings.

We ended up meeting later in the day for a drink. I was feeling bold and validated by my morning date with a guy who said nice things and told me I was beautiful and that he had been intimidated by my "It Girl" status back in high school. This was like a rush of ego sugar through my veins and to my brain. *Maybe I still have it. Maybe I'm still worthy.*

I met Married Man at a bar and made him look me in the eye and tell me he chose *her* over *me*. Chose staying over leaving. Wanted him to tell me he didn't love me. Dared him to say it didn't matter. Begged him to hurt me. I wanted closure, sweet painful closure.

But he wouldn't give it to me. He was still wishy-washy, undecided, stuck.

"You made a choice," I challenged him to own his actions.
"I know, I know, but …"

And with each *but* I heard *but I really want you. I love you. I choose you. You do matter. You are special.* He wouldn't even give me the satisfaction of letting me go. Again. Texted me later that night saying he had forgotten how "smokin' hot" I was. And I allowed myself to imagine he cared. Really and truly. That his empty words meant something. That I meant something to him.

A day or two later he texted again, "I'd like to tie you up and teach you a lesson."

And I remembered what a pig he was. Truly.

Married Man wanted a blow-up doll to play out his macho fantasies. Someone to objectify and control. Just like Pazzo. I wasn't even a real person to him. I was a means to an end.

Red flag.

Then there was the recovering heroin addict/sexy waiter, 20-plus years my junior who lied about everything, and ultimately threw me under the bus for the psycho, stalker girlfriend I never knew he had. The text thread went something like this:

This is Liam's girlfriend can you please call back right away?
Why are you calling my boyfriend
Who the fuck is this
Who are you
And how do you know him
And why the fuck are you texting him like this
It's Liam I need to call you I need you to answer
Can you please call me so we can clear this up with my girlfriend.
Just want to reassure her that this is a mistake and that there is nothing going on between us.

Sexy Waiter wasn't overtly cruel, just dishonest, neglectful, and unreliable, chronically late or MIA. All traits of an addict. Oh, and he was dating someone else, unbeknownst to me. We weren't exclusive. I was under no illusions. But apparently his girlfriend was.

He had this indefinable sweetness about him, a fragile innocence and vulnerability I found refreshing after Pazzo's impenetrable armor of utter contempt. Sexy Waiter was childlike in certain ways. And eager to please.

We were sitting outside one evening, talking and watching the sun go down, when he got up and went inside and came back out with a broom. Then he swept my deck. Every leaf, every twig. Meticulously and intentionally. He made sure to only sweep the leaves into the beds below, not onto the walkway. It was the dearest thing ever. Just an unselfish act of thoughtfulness. And I loved him for it.

He'd smoke, then line his cigarette butts up like so many snuffed out dreams.

I wanted to save fix him somehow. Remember, I'm a pleaser and a fixer. Or maybe I saw something of my former self in him, my own lost innocence. But in the end, all Sexy Waiter wanted was to take something from me, although I'm still not sure what. What need did I fill that his girlfriend didn't? What hurt did I kiss all better?

They were all needy and self-absorbed, these men I chose after Pazzo, And I made them feel better about themselves. I was a mirror that reflected a flattering view of the people they wished they were. I made them feel seen, heard, and understood—the threefold human hunger. *The light in me sees, hears, and understands the light in you.*

But it wasn't enough. They were takers, parasites, feeding

on my energy and eating my heart out. Sexual predators. Soul vampires. Charming, intelligent, charismatic, contemptuous. There was some Pazzo in all of them. It's a pattern of abuse I'd like to break, even if it means giving up on love, at least in that narrow sense of the word.

When people show you who they are, believe them. Believe in patterns not apologies. Heed the warning signs. Notice the *red flags*. And leave behind what isn't good for you. I'm saying this as much for myself as I am for you. Because even after Pazzo, I'm still vulnerable to seduction, to the wonderful numbing out of it. Just as Sexy Waiter numbed out with heroin, my drug of choice is that fleeting rush of infatuation, that jolt of endorphins, that false feeling of absolute acceptance fueled by the illusion of adoration by someone else.

I read once about lab rats or hamsters or some other doomed rodent that had a choice between an endorphin rush—stimulated by pushing a button—or food. The poor little creatures chose ecstasy over sustenance every time. Eventually starved to death in their tiny cages.

I recently found a sand dollar on the beach. It was broken in half, but the two halves had been carefully placed beside each other on a piece of driftwood, where I happened to sit for a moment during my walk. I glanced down and saw the fragile, chalky pieces glowing against the calm gray of the weathered wood. Upon closer examination, I noticed that the delicate, damaged halves were touching at one edge and pulling apart from each other on the other edge. The sand dollar looked like pie, with a sliver gone.

I was left to wonder at the care someone had taken to

align the pieces but not to put them all the way back together again. It seemed emblematic of my love life. Ripped asunder and never quite fitting back together. Or maybe the two halves weren't even from the same sand dollar in the first place. While a circle is a beautiful organic shape with magical properties, maybe I'm not meant to find another half to complete me. Maybe I'm not that kind of sea creature after all.

In a world where everyone wears a mask, it's a privilege to see a soul.

Truth from a Facebook meme.

The other day I opened the obituary section of the paper. I was sitting in Starbucks, scanning for the deaths of parents of my childhood friends, as has become my habit these days. Those of us new members of the Orphan Club have an invisible connection to our fellow orphans-to-be. I once read that you're not truly an adult until you've lost both of your parents. Adulting is hard.

My eyes stopped at a particular entry. Elise Pazzo.

My throat closed like his hands were around it.

There was the same lovely profile picture of her from Facebook. Her wedding day photo when her whole future was in front of her, her new life with her "best friend." She was two days shy of her 37nd birthday when her life was snuffed out.

I tried to slow my beating heart. I feared everyone in Starbucks could hear it pounding as I read. Elise had died "suddenly" and was survived by "her devoted and adoring husband, Dr. Michael Pazzo. I could tell he had written the obit. Elise was described as a breath of fresh air, beloved by her friends and all who knew her. "Her laughter was like music; her smile was the sun." The hyperbole was over the top. And I knew then that she had not gone willingly, or quietly, or peacefully. I pictured a pillow over her face or a staged suicide of pill-strewn sheets.

Or perhaps even something more gruesome. Remember the scene in *Hannibal* when Anthony Hopkins' sociopathic antagonist talks his drugged victim into slicing the skin off his own face with a piece of broken mirror? Could Pazzo have coaxed his pretty, young wife into a bathtub of warm water, plied her with red wine and Xanax and convinced her to slit her wrists, filling the Jacuzzi with blood the color of her Pinot Noir? Or maybe she fell asleep in the steamy blanket of soothing water, and he just pulled her toes till her face slipped beneath the surface.

And is he, even as we speak, cruising online dating sites, like a shark in the water smelling blood, searching for his next victim, his next wife, his next Colleen. Someone to lure and charm and capture and control and, ultimately, consume and destroy.

Life doesn't go in a straight line. It's a series of twists and turns, cutbacks and climbs. You evolve and adapt along the way, reinventing yourself, chameleon-like, as the scenery changes. Your essence remains, but it manifests differently in different settings.

I've sold my little cottage where I landed after condo life—Hank needed a backyard—and I'm driving toward the coast to live closer to the sea, where I'm most at home. This restless mermaid is on the move, drawn by the smell of saltwater and the rhythm of the waves.

You cannot always wait for the perfect time. Sometimes you must dare to jump. I read that on Twitter, and it feels right.

Tell me, what is it you plan to do with your one wild and precious life? I don't know the answer to the question Mary Oliver poses in her gorgeous poem, but I aim to find out.

I hope I don't get a package in the mail, stilettos and champagne corks, bunny faces on the mailing label. But if I do, I'll burn it and sprinkle the ashes over the ocean and forgive myself for letting a monster into my life that I can never be rid of.

Because in this moment, I have the power to say this is not how my story ends.

About the Author

Laura Mansfield is a brand journalist with one of the top independent advertising agencies in the country. Fluent in social media, she has a digital mindset, a great appreciation for words, a flair for storytelling, and a love of good conversation.

She is also the author of the Number 1 Amazon.com bestseller,

Geezer Stories: The Care and Feeding of Old People

The Narcissist's Wife is her first novel.
Laura writes from her home in East Tennessee.

Also Available From

WordCrafts Press

The 5 Manners of Death
  by Darden North

Ill Gotten Gain
  by Ralph E. Jarrells

The Mirror Lies
  by Sandy Brownlee

Devil's Charm
  by Leslie Conner

End of Summer
  by Michael Potts

Odd Man Outlaw
  by K.M. Zahrt

Made in the USA
Monee, IL
05 June 2022

97495658R00094